NIG

Dying to Dance

Someone had followed me inside the building. Fear prickled through my nerves as I ran up the steps. Fumbling with my keys, I searched for the one to the studio door. If I can just get inside and lock the door behind me, I'll call the police and...

Then my eyes fell on the shiny new lock, and the bottom fell out of my stomach. I didn't have a key to the new lock. I couldn't get in. I was trapped.

Footsteps moved cautiously up the stairs towards me. Heavy steps, trying to be quiet...

More heart-stopping Nightmares...

NIGHTMARES

Dying to Dance

Nicole Davidson

HarperCollins*Publishers*

First published in the USA by Avon Books in 1996
First published in Great Britain in 1996
by HarperCollins*Publishers* Ltd.,
77-85 Fulham Palace Road, Hammersmith, London W6 8JB

1 3 5 7 9 8 6 4 2

Printed and bound in Great Britain by
Caledonian International Book Manufacturing Ltd,
Glasgow G64

As soon as I turned out the lights, I heard the sound again. It was very soft, only a gentle scraping noise, like someone trying to scratch a label off of a glass jar.

I moved my hand slowly away from the light switch and squinted at the dark room, trying to locate the source of the noise. Nothing, that I could see, was moving.

With the lights off, the mirrors surrounding the main teaching room in the dance studio dimly reflected the street lamps outside. Tall windows along one side overlooked Allegheny Street, while the other three sides of the room were floor-to-ceiling mirrors—to let students and teachers see themselves while they danced. They also made the area look more spacious. The studio was a lot smaller than my parents had hoped it would be when they'd opened the Dying to Dance Studio ten years before.

Tonight, though, the place felt enormous and empty around me and, in a vague way I couldn't quite put my finger on, threatening! Empty, that is, except for that noise . . . because *something* had to be making it. I wanted to leave and get home as fast as I could.

1

Running, I could make it in fifteen minutes, maybe less.

But since my parents trusted me to lock up on weeknights when I stayed late, I knew I shouldn't leave until I'd located the sound and made sure it wasn't rats or my brother's pet snake, Alfred, whom he'd misplaced over a year ago and we'd never found. (My parents made us swear we'd never tell any of the students about Alfred.)

I heard it again—soft, controlled scratchings. Each sharp scrape sent a wave of shivers up my spine.

Spinning around, I caught a blurry reflection of myself in the surrounding mirrors: a tall, slim teenage girl in jeans with blonde hair pulled back in a ponytail, tiptoeing stealthily toward the other side of the room. A hundred Carrie Clarks trailed after me across the waxed wooden floor. Each step I took dragged them along, as reluctant as I was to look into the two smaller practice rooms.

Nothing was in either one.

I strained, listening for the sound again—there. I held my breath. *There* it was!

Jerking around once again, I felt my heart pound like a pep band drum in my chest, my fingertips moist with nervous sweat. The scratchings were definitely coming from just outside the studio door, in the third-floor hallway near the elevator.

Clutching my purse and the keys, I ran across the ballroom floor, past the desk where my mother always sat, welcoming students to their lessons, answering the phone, and explaining over and over, "No, we don't offer ballet or tap lessons. But we can teach you to waltz or tango beautifully."

I walked slower as I neared the hall door.

A frosted glass pane filled the upper half of the

2

door. My eyes latched onto the swirly, black letters—
DTD—painted backward to show from the outside. I
took the last few steps and reached cautiously for the
doorknob.

"Who's there?" I called out, trying to sound au-
thoritative.

A shadow flashed across the glass. Steps thundered
down the stairwell.

Oh god, I thought, *someone was trying to break in!*

For a long moment I stood leaning against the wall,
trying to stop my heart from hammering clear through
my ribs, working at catching my breath. Then I dove
for the telephone and punched in 9-1-1.

Pulling in a sharp breath, I opened my mouth to
shout out the address and anything else that would get
the cops there fast. A fraction of a second later, I
changed my mind. I hung up before the operator could
answer.

"This is really stupid," I muttered to myself.

Of course I should report that someone had been
lurking in the hallway. But over the years I'd learned
the lengths that parents could go in cases like this. If
I freaked out over a shadow in the hallway after hours,
I would be the one to suffer.

I lifted the receiver again and dialed home.

"Clark residence," my mother answered in her
smooth, professional voice.

"Hi Mom," I chirped. "Is Andy there?"

"Oh hi, sweetheart. Are you still at the studio?"
She sounded as if her mind was on something else. I
could hear water running and dishes clinking. My parents often ate dinner at 11:00 P.M., after lessons were
over. "It's getting late," she added, "for a school
night."

"I know. I have a lot of homework, but I also

3

wanted to practice a step that's got me hammered. I need to talk to Andy."

"I'll get him," she said.

I drummed my fingers on the desktop, keeping an eye on the frosted glass, listening deeply for the sound of returning steps in the stairwell.

"Yeah, what's up?"

"Come down here, fast," I rasped at my brother through the receiver.

He laughed. "No way am I leaving this house. I've got two midterms tomorrow. I need the study time."

"I need you to . . . to . . . work on a step with me." If I told him the real reason, he'd rat to Mom and Dad. But I didn't want to leave the building alone. "It's very important—part of the waltz routine for the Mid-Atlantic comps."

Andy and I had competed in ballroom competitions since we were in grade school. It wasn't a romantic thing at all—and not just because we're brother and sister. Professional dancing isn't at all like what you see in the movies—*Dirty Dancing, Strictly Ballroom*, or even those old Fred Astaire and Ginger Rogers flicks where the guy whisks his starry-eyed partner across the floor as she falls in love with him.

No way.

What we did required hours of exhausting athletic training. It was every bit as tough as playing forward on the girl's varsity basketball team, which I'd done for two years so I know.

Although I never thought of dancing as fun or romantic, it did make me feel special in a way I'd never been able to explain to even my closest friends. The music . . . the throb of the bass beat seeping up through the soles of my shoes . . . the way my body moved almost without my telling it to . . .

4

Dancing was me and I was it. I could no longer separate the two. Like Siamese twins, we were destined to spend life together.

There were some cool benefits, though. There's no higher high than hearing your name called out by the judges before an audience of hundreds of people: "Carrie and Andy Clark, first place in International waltz, junior division!" The crowd goes wild, clapping and screaming, as we walk across the ballroom, under chandeliers dripping with crystal, and accept the trophy from the judge . . .

I'll never get enough of that feeling of being the best at something.

That feeling of knowing only a few people in the world can do what you do . . . and do it that well . . .

"Carrie? Carrie, are you there? I said, I'm not coming over there, and I mean it!"

I blinked, remembering why I'd called Andy. "This is *very* important." I hissed into the phone. "It's not about the comp. There's a problem at the studio, and I don't want Mom and Dad to flip out. Get down here now. I'll let you in."

I hung up and stared at the phone, half expecting it to ring. Andy would either call back and tell me to quit bugging him, or he'd be on his way by now.

The phone didn't ring.

I hunched down on the floor just inside the door, watching the glass pane, hoping the next shadow I saw would be my brother's.

5

2 **Andy made it to the studio** in four minutes, so I knew he'd taken his car. His footsteps rumbled up the stairs—as only his did—two steps at a time.

"Hey, you in there or what!" he shouted, when I didn't have the door open for him.

I swung it wide, never so glad to see my big brother.

We looked a lot alike—sandy blond hair and hazel eyes that changed with the weather. We were both tall too. Andy, a senior at H. L. Mencken High, was six-foot-one, and I was five-eleven, standing above most of the other girls in the junior class, dwarfing half the boys, too.

I didn't care. Our height made it easy for the judges to pick us out of a crowd of contestants during preliminaries. Andy and I always made the cuts, and we usually placed in the top three couples for the finals.

We nearly crashed into each other as he rushed into the studio and I ran past him into the hallway.

"Where are you going?" he demanded. "I thought there was something wrong in the studio."

"There is . . . or was," I corrected myself. "I just have to see something."

Stooping outside the door, I studied the keyhole in the middle of the brass knob. Around it were tiny, bright scratch marks. Marks that, I was sure, hadn't been there before.

"See?" I said, satisfied that I hadn't been imagining things.

"What?"

I stood up. "Someone was tampering with the lock, trying to break into the studio."

Andy squinted at me, then at the door. "So why didn't you call the police?"

"I started to, then I remembered what Mom and Dad would do if they found out. They'd never let me stay after hours again."

"So what?"

I groaned. Why did he need an explanation for everything? "So, I *need* some time to myself, you know that. You take off and drive around in your car when you want some space. It's the same thing. This is the only place I can be alone." He didn't look convinced. "I can't stand having them looking over my shoulder all the time, interrogating me about my homework, listening in on every telephone conversation I have with Diana or Tammy."

"I guess . . ." Andy shrugged, looking as if he'd lost interest. He glanced down at the lock and touched the scratches. "Well, it was probably just kids, fooling around. There isn't much worth stealing here."

I nodded. What he'd said was true. Still, just the idea of some stranger coming through the door while I was there alone gave me the creeps.

"Let's get going," he said. "I've got a lot to do tonight."

I reached out and grabbed his arm. "Wait. Since

7

you're here, we might as well work on that one step for our jive routine.''

Jive was like swing dancing, "hand dancing," as kids around here called it. A few under twenty-one clubs had sprung up, and the high school and college crowd jammed them, while the deejay mixed fast-paced swing with alternative rock.

Andy looked away from me. "I have to talk to you about *that*."

"What? The routine? You don't like it?"

"No," he said, looking uncomfortable. "I mean, I have to talk to you about the Mid-Atlantics next month. I'm not going to be able to dance with you, Carrie."

I was sure I hadn't heard him right. "Is something wrong? If you don't like the costumes or the music, we can change them."

He shook his head, staring down at his hands. "No. It's just that . . ." He rolled his eyes. "Hey, we've been doing this stuff since I was seven years old and you were six, for crying out loud. Maybe that's enough."

I couldn't believe what I was hearing. "You want to break up the team, quit dancing?" I gasped. The words felt impossible on my tongue.

"Not exactly," he said slowly. "I just think I need a change. I want to dance for myself for a change. You know, have fun, not work so hard at it."

"We could cut back on rehearsals, if you think we can get away with less practice time."

Andy spun around and stared at me, his gray-green eyes snapping with anger. "You don't get it, do you?" he asked tightly. "I don't want to dance with my *sister* any more."

Then I knew where he was headed, and I backed

8

away, viewing him between the narrowed slits of my eyelids. "You traitor," I growled. "You creep! You're not going to dance with Miranda, are you?"

"Well . . ." he began sheepishly.

I glared at him, my own anger overshadowing his. "That egotistical, cheating—"

He held up his hands in protest. "Now, Carrie, she's a good dancer, you have to admit, and she likes to win . . . just like you. That doesn't make her a bad person."

"She's been chasing after you for years!" I shouted at him. "Every time one of her partners walks out on her, she comes running to you."

Andy ignored me. "Come on, you got everything you need? Let's go home."

Still fuming, I ran back into the instructors' dressing room and snatched up my bookbag. Giving the room a quick once-over to make sure the cleaning job I'd finished an hour ago was good enough to pass my mother's inspection, I ran to join my traitor brother. I locked the hallway door after us.

"You think it will be okay to just leave the place and not call the police?" I asked.

"Like I said, it was probably just kids messing around. If a pro had been breaking in, you wouldn't have heard a thing. He'd have been through that door in five seconds."

"Very reassuring," I mumbled.

We took the elevator down. It was old and creaky, only big enough for three people, and it ran three times as fast going down as up.

Andy's Ford Escort was parked on the street. I slumped in the passenger seat, mulling over his decision while he drove, and getting angrier by the second.

9

"If you think she really likes you, you're crazy," I blurted out.

"Miranda?" he asked innocently.

"Yes, Miranda. Sexy Miranda Hemingway with her long black hair and flirty eyes and slinky figure and—"

"Enough, Carrie," he muttered.

"I mean it. She's just using you, Andy. I know you've had a crush on her forever. But she doesn't care if you get hurt, as long as you'll dance with her. She knows she'll have a great shot at winning with you as her partner."

He smiled across the car at me and ruffled my hair. "Hey, thanks for the compliment."

I groaned. "Come on, be reasonable. If we take the regionals next month, we could have a shot at a national title in January. We could do it! We really could!"

I watched his expression, and could see a flicker of indecision. Then his eyes hardened with determination, the same way they did just before a performance. "No," he said. "I've already told her I'll do it. Anyway, it's what I want. I need a change."

The Escort pulled into the driveway behind my father's gray sedan.

"What am I going to do for a partner?" I murmured, feeling totally miserable.

He looked at me. "Jay Silverberg?"

"He's three inches shorter than I am. We'd look ridiculous together."

"Ben Green?"

"He's thirty years old, for crying out loud!" I shouted at him.

He climbed out of the car and there was nothing for me to do but get out and follow him toward the house.

"Look, I'm sorry, Carrie," he said over his shoulder. "I know you'll find someone, if you want to make the comp. I just can't do it with you any more."

A sudden, desperate chill fell over me. I knew what I had to do, even though it was playing dirty. "Have you told Mom and Dad?"

Andy froze, his foot on the second step leading up to the porch. "No."

If I ran inside crying to them this very minute, if I sobbed to my mother how Andy had destroyed my career by turning traitor and dancing with Miranda Hemingway, I knew they'd make him dance the next comp with me. But I also knew Andy would hate me forever, and I'd still be faced with finding someone to dance with for the nationals, because they wouldn't make him stay with me forever.

Andy turned and looked at me. "I was going to tell them next week, after Miranda and I have our routines worked out a little better. Then we could show them what we have planned."

I nodded, biting back more threats. Bitter tears burned my eyes.

"Are you going to say anything to them?" he asked.

"No," I forced out. "I guess not."

I went straight upstairs to my room and collapsed on my bed, disgusted with my life. I wished with all my heart that Miranda Hemingway were dead.

3 "I wish Miranda were dead!" I said out loud in the middle of the social studies wing of Mencken High.

A couple of kids passing by me and my best friends, Diana and Tammy, looked our way and grinned. Who knows, maybe they'd had the same thought about Miranda, like a couple of hundred times.

Diana grinned at me. "Hey, I could arrange that! See, I've got a cousin who knows a guy who once took money to beat up this golfer before a big match, and—"

"Carrie's kidding, you idiot!" Tammy snapped at her. She turned to me, anxiously twirling the long strand of beads that hung around her neck. This month she was into Native American jewelry. "You wouldn't *really* want anything bad to happen to Miranda, would you?"

"Nothing worse than a collision with a Mack truck." I sighed, playing with the gold chain bracelet on my wrist. "I guess not. Not really. It would just make things a lot simpler. Andy has this sickening crush on her. If she weren't around, I don't think he'd have any interest in dancing with anyone but me."

Diana looked appropriately distressed on my behalf. "So does this mean you're giving up dancing in competitions?"

"No," I said, firmly. "I'll find someone . . . someone good, someone tall, some guy who can dance circles around Andy and . . . and his new partner." I couldn't force myself to say Miranda's name one more time.

A bunch of guys from the basketball team walked past, and Diana giggled. "Any of them are tall enough for you."

"They'd never dance with her," Tammy said.

"Why not?" I asked.

"Get real," Tammy said. "Jocks? You know what they think of your kind of dancing. None of them would be caught dead on a ballroom floor in a tuxedo."

Yet the guys had stopped hassling Andy about dancing back in eighth grade. That was when he'd punched out Joel White for calling him a sissy.

"You're right," I agreed, catching the eyes of one of the boys.

He had chocolate-brown hair and was wearing what everyone else wore these days—baggy jeans and a rumpled flannel shirt over a dark-colored T-shirt. I didn't know his name. I knew his friends, though. Micky Johnson and Ralph Sanders had gone to school with me since fourth grade. They were as macho as macho could get. I couldn't see either one of them doing an advanced hip twist.

I sighed. "I'll have to talk to my parents next week, after Andy breaks the news to them. Maybe they'll have some ideas."

* * *

All day long, the only thing I could think about was Andy's plans to dance with Miranda. I reached the studio that afternoon before remembering about the kids trying to break in. Guiltily, I glanced at my mother as I walked in the door. I'd almost slipped past her to the dressing room when she looked up from her paperwork.

"Just a minute, young lady."

Great, I thought, *she noticed the scratch marks on the door knob.*

"Something wrong, Mom?" I asked innocently.

"Yes, something's *very* wrong."

Oops. "I'm sorry, I didn't want you to know. I thought you'd be upset."

"Of course I'm upset. Who wouldn't be?"

I ducked my head, trying to look penitent. "Sorry. Did you call the police?"

She frowned at me. "Police?"

"Yeah, to report what happened."

Now she really looked suspicious. "I may have been tempted, at times, to have you arrested when you didn't pick up after yourself, but I don't believe I'd ever actually do it."

"Huh?" It took a minute for her words to sink in. "*Pick up after myself.*"

She sighed. "Carrie, you know perfectly well you were supposed to tidy up the dressing room before you left last night."

"I did."

She stood up and looked down the endless length of her nose at me, and pointed toward the dressing room. With a groan I tromped across the reception area. Apparently I hadn't done the job to her satisfaction. Maybe I should have taken the time to vacuum.

I stopped in the doorway and stared into the room

where the instructors changed their clothes and left their personal things while they taught. It looked as if a hurricane had dropped down through the ceiling, lingered for twenty minutes, then left a trail of destruction behind it.

The closet, holding costumes my mom and dad had worn when they'd danced in comps before I'd been born and while I was growing up, hung open. Three of my own gowns had been in there, too, but the red, sequin-spangled Latin outfit was lying in a heap on the floor, looking as if it was cringing away from the hands that had torn it off its hanger. My collection of CDs and tapes was spilled across the floor. The cushions had been dragged off the couch and scattered.

I heard footsteps behind me. My mother, I guessed, closing in for the kill.

"If you call this tidying up, young lady—"

"Mom, this is terrible!"

"I'll say it is."

"No, you don't understand!" I twisted around to face her. "I didn't do this! I really *did* pick up last night. Everything was in order when I left with Andy. I swear."

She frowned, as if for the first time realizing the illogic of my throwing around my own stuff, which I'd worked so hard to buy. My ballroom costumes, even though they were secondhand, cost hundreds of dollars each. And I'd started my CD collection when I was a little kid, cautiously spending the allowance I earned by sweeping the studio floors and answering the phone for my parents when they were teaching.

An icy chill inched up my spine. Whoever had been trying to get into the studio last night had come back.

I knew I couldn't keep the intruder a secret any longer. "Mom, I think you'd better check the rest of the studio. Someone obviously broke in here last night.''

She surveyed the room again, her lips slowly turning downward, the color rushing from her cheeks. ''Oh, I don't think . . . but the door was locked when we opened up this afternoon.''

I shook my head. ''Anyone can turn the button from the inside then step outside and pull the door closed.''

She nodded. ''I'll check the petty cash box and my office.''

I followed her out into the reception area and watched her open the middle drawer, guessing what she'd find . . . or, rather, not find.

''The cash box is gone,'' she murmured, then bit down on her lower lip. ''Go back into my office and use the other line to call your father at home.'' She was already reaching for the phone on the receptionist's desk. ''I'll notify the police.''

A Baltimore County officer showed up twenty minutes later. After my father explained what seemed to have happened the night before, the cop asked the three of us to walk him through the studio. We started in the reception area, then set off for the first practice room.

''Anything missing in here?'' he asked.

My father shook his head.

''In here?'' he asked in the next practice room.

''No,'' my mother said. ''The only thing that seems to be actually missing, so far, is the cash box. There was fifty dollars in change and small bills. I'd dropped off the lesson money in the night deposit at Maryland National.''

My father had been very quiet. He looked at me.

16

"I'm just glad Carrie left before this person broke in."

The cop turned to me. His name tag read MILLER. "You were here alone last night, miss?"

"Yes." I explained how I often stayed late to practice, or work on the choreography for a new dance routine, or just to play CDs while doing my homework. "I can turn up the volume real loud and not disturb anyone," I said. "May I pick up my CDs and costume now?" I asked.

"Let me take a look in there first," he said.

My father coughed lightly and glanced at my mother. "Officer, we have students coming in. I don't want to alarm them. Can you and Carrie manage all right while we get the next class started?"

"Sure," he said. "I'll come get you if I need you."

The cop and I walked into the dressing room. He was young and, I thought, sort of cute. As he looked around, he made a few more notes on a form he'd been carrying around. "Is anything missing in here?"

"I don't think so." But I had over a hundred CDs, so it would take me a while to put them all in order and run inventory.

"Why don't you take a closer look around, just to be sure," he suggested.

I started scooping up plastic cases, stacking them beside the wooden rack Andy had made for me in woodworking shop at school. There seemed to be an awful lot of them, but as I mentally sorted, noticing which ones I'd already come across, I began to get a funny feeling in the pit of my stomach.

"What's wrong?" the cop asked.

"I-I'm not sure," I stammered. "I haven't found two of my favorites. One CD had my new routine on it."

17

He stooped and started gathering up more cases. "What are the names of the missing ones?"

I told him, and together we started a faster, more focused search. After ten minutes, we'd gone through all of the CDs, and we still hadn't found them.

I told him the names again, so he could note them on his report, then I looked up into the closet. There was a space where the Latin costume had been hanging. "Can I pick up my clothes now too?"

"Sure."

I reached for the crimson stretch-satin leotard decorated with hand-sewn bugle beads, sequins, and fringe. When I picked it up, it didn't feel right. I turned the fabric over in my hands.

"Oh no-o-o-o," I breathed.

"What is it?" He looked up from his paper.

"Look." I held the costume up for him.

The shoulder straps had been torn loose, and the skirt was shredded, yanked free in two spots at the hips. His expression was a blank, as if he wasn't sure what it was *supposed* to look like.

"It's ruined," I choked out, my throat closing up as I tried to fight back my rage and tears.

He nodded toward the closet. "What about the rest of the stuff?"

I dropped the red fabric and raced to the closet. Quickly, I slid each costume along the pole, checking for tears, missing sleeves, or any other damage. "Everything seems to be all right," I reported at last. Then it hit me.

I flipped through the dresses one more time, then again as a lump grew in my throat.

"Something missing?" he asked.

"Yes," I ground out. "Yes, my new gown for the competition next month!" The competition I probably

18

wasn't going to be able to dance in anyway, because my selfish brother had ditched me. "It was peach colored, with lace sleeves and matching ostrich feathers all around the bottom of a long, full skirt."

"You're sure it didn't fall on the closet floor or get jammed behind the others?"

"No!" I moaned, tears springing to my eyes. "It's gone!"

4 "I think it's kind of exciting," Diana stated the next day in school. "The cops investigating at the studio, and all."

"It stinks," I muttered. "First Andy quits on me and now my gown is missing. I don't think there's any way I can dance in the Mid-Atlantics."

"Maybe the police will find out who broke in and get your CDs and dress back," Tammy said hopefully.

She was wearing a different necklace today. A few weeks before, she'd started making them as a hobby. Stringing beads was very calming, she'd told me.

Diana was the opposite. She never wore any kind of jewelry and preferred total grungewear—the more holes in her jeans, the better.

"Or maybe you could make a new gown," Tammy suggested as an afterthought. "I'll help."

My mom and I had sewn the peach gown. "It took us three months the first time, and the materials cost me four hundred dollars," I said glumly. "There's no way. I just wish I knew who'd done this."

Diana nudged me with her flannel-covered elbow. "I have a pretty good guess."

I looked up. Diana was staring across the hallway at Miranda Hemingway, who was rummaging around in her locker.

No, I thought, *even Miranda wouldn't stoop that low.*

Or would she?

Just then Miranda turned and saw me. Her dark eyes flashed, and the corners of her lips turned up in a taunting smile. *Loser,* she mouthed.

I thrust my books into Diana's arms and started across the hallway.

"Where are you going?" Tammy called after me. "Carrie, don't—"

But I'd stopped listening to my friends. Anger bubbled up inside of me like lava frothing out of a volcano. With every step I took, I was more and more sure that I was right. Of course, it had to be Miranda. First she snatched Andy, then my dress and my music. The witch!

I was beside her before she could close her locker. "I want my things back," I demanded.

Miranda coolly snapped the combination lock shut and turned to face me, her eyes wide as if she were honestly puzzled. "Carrie, hi. What things?"

"My gown and CDs . . . you know very well. You took them."

She laughed, but looked up and down the hall as if hoping to spot a passing teacher, just in case she needed protection. "I don't know what you're talking about."

"Someone broke into the studio last night and stole my new gown and some of my music. Why would an ordinary thief want a ballroom gown?" I glared at her accusingly.

Miranda shrugged. "To spruce up her wardrobe?"

Looking pleased with herself, she started to turn away.

This was just the kind of mean trick she'd pull. We always danced in the same comps, and she inevitably found some way to make a fuss with the judges— point out a step Andy and I had done that she didn't think was on the syllabus, to get us disqualified; demand she be allowed a second chance to perform because the buckle on her shoe had broken. Once, she'd intentionally spilled some soda on the waxed floor, but I'd seen her do it and warned Andy to avoid the spot.

Anyway, Andy and I had always beaten her, before now . . .

But I'd run out of patience with her.

"I know you did it!" I shouted in her face, grabbing her arm and shaking it hard. "First you steal Andy, then you pull this."

"Let go, Carrie, you're hurting me," she whimpered.

I looked down at my hand to see my fingernails biting into the creamy flesh of her forearm. A small crowd of students had gathered around us, curious to see what was going on.

I didn't care, didn't pay any attention to them. An angry red haze blotted out their faces. A calming voice close to my ear, that I sensed must be Diana's, only irritated me more. I blocked out what she was saying and shoved her aside.

"You stay away from the studio," I snarled at Miranda, at last releasing her. "You leave us alone, or I'll . . . I'll make you sorry. I swear I'll get you!"

Miranda rubbed her arm and glared at me as she took a backward step. Arching one dark brow at me, she whispered, "You haven't got a chance now, Carrie. Admit it. I hold all the cards."

I longed to grab her around the throat and squeeze and squeeze and squeeze . . . until that stupid, self-satisfied grin fell from her face. But I made myself turn away and march down the hall into the girls' lavatory.

After splashing a couple of gallons of cold water on my face, I finally stopped crying. I was shaking all over, shaking so hard my bones hurt. I'd never felt so out of control before.

But when I thought about all the years Miranda had been mean to me, all the times she'd hurt my feelings and been rotten to my friends—and now convinced Andy to dance with her—one blowup didn't seem that outrageous.

I looked up into the mirror and Diana was standing there, waiting for me with a pained expression on her pretty face. "You all right?" she whispered.

"I guess."

"I thought you were going to kill her right there in front of all those kids. I've never seen you so mad."

"I thought I was going to, too." I sighed. "Nothing is going right. Nothing at all."

"Come on," she said gently. "We'll be late for class. After school, I'll walk you to the studio. On the way we can think up ways to bump off Miranda, without witnesses. Ever consider dynamite?"

I rolled my tear-swollen eyes. "Very funny."

"Well," she said, "maybe we can at least come up with a way to find you a partner. You can always wear one of your old costumes, right?"

"Yeah." I smiled at her gratefully, but didn't feel much better. The only comfort I found was a grim phrase that kept tumbling through my mind: *The only good Miranda is a dead Miranda.*

Well, at least I could fantasize.

A locksmith was working on the entry door of the studio in the third-floor hallway when I arrived at Dying to Dance that afternoon. He'd installed a brass security plate around the doorknob and was finishing up with a dead bolt strong enough to keep a herd of elephants from stampeding through.

I was already in a rotten mood when I walked past him into the reception area. Then Mom reminded me we were starting a new Wedding Survival class at 7:00 P.M.

"Your father wants you to help him teach tonight's session," she informed me.

I opened my mouth to object, but the phone rang. She reached for the receiver and immediately started talking to someone about signing up for lessons.

"I hate working with beginners," I muttered, slinging my bookbag over my shoulder and heading for the dressing room.

Suddenly I was reminded of the break in, and nothing else seemed very important. I had to find out if we had another copy of my music. Not that it really mattered for the comps, since the organizers of each competition chose whatever pieces they wanted. But some kinds of music were more inspiring than others, and I could get lost in a mesmerizing rhythm. That was the kind I liked for practicing.

Diana had been right. I could always wear one of my old costumes. I wouldn't make quite as dramatic a picture in the white gown I'd worn for the last four years and nearly outgrown. But Mom always said,

"It's your dancing, not your dress, the judges will be scoring."

I knew that was true . . . but the peach gown had been so very beautiful. My heart nearly broke thinking of it. Maybe the police would find it. I wondered if I should tell them to look in Miranda's closet—the snake!

I should have started right in on my English Lit reading, but I spent two hours on the phone, calling everyone I knew to try to find a new partner. I had to be careful how I asked, because of Andy's decision not to tell Mom and Dad until the following week.

"Why are you interested in another professional male dancer?" Mrs. Zvorsky at the Fred Astaire studio in Baltimore asked. "You have Andy, right?"

"Oh sure," I fibbed. "I'm just asking for a friend. She's from out of town and might be moving here." Everyone involved in professional ballroom dancing knew everyone else, so I had to be vague.

"Well, there's always Ben Green, although he's a little old. She couldn't dance in the juniors' category."

"I know," I said. "Can't you think of any other pros in the area?" I pleaded. "Or even amateurs . . . you know, some guy who's been taking lessons with you for years, who seems talented, picks up steps easily . . ."

I could imagine her shaking her head and wondering why I sounded so desperate. "No, dear, sorry. Not even my advanced students are capable of dancing on your level . . . your friend's level, that is. She'd be laughed off the dance floor at a comp."

I squeezed my eyes shut. "Thanks for trying anyway," I murmured and hung up.

I called four other coaches—two in Baltimore, two

25

in Washington, D.C., which was close enough to drive to in an hour. The only names they mentioned were those of guys I'd seen dance before and knew weren't for me. Either our heights didn't match, or they were on ego trips, or they just weren't very good. I doubted if my parents could come up with anyone on such short notice, even if I had been able to confide in them.

At 6:00 P.M., I gave up and ran across the street to Donna's Sandwich Shop to grab some supper and bring back stuff for Mom and Dad. Andy hadn't shown up after school. I couldn't remember if he was working at the mall today or not. My brother had worked at the Athlete's Foot in the Towsontowne Mall for two years. *Maybe he's practicing with Miranda*, I thought glumly.

But as I was crossing the street, I spotted Miranda walking alone down the sidewalk. I was about to change directions to avoid running into her, when she stepped inside Vivaldi's Collectibles, the antique shop owned by her aunt.

Miranda worked there a few hours every week. I suspected she mostly sat behind the counter, read magazines, and collected her paycheck as if it were an allowance.

I cursed her under my breath and dashed into Donna's, with less appetite than I'd had five minutes earlier.

By 7:00 P.M. a class of ten adults had gathered in a nervous knot around my mother's desk. All of the men looked as if they'd rather jump naked into a snake pit. The women chattered in high-pitched voices among themselves, while keeping one eye on their fiancés to make sure they didn't make a run for the stairs.

I rolled my eyes at my father. "Do I *have* to?" I whispered.

He nodded solemnly, then turned to the class members. "Come on into the ballroom, folks. We'll get started now."

They trooped after him like obedient children, and I reluctantly brought up what I thought was the rear.

"Hey, you taking this dumb class too?" a deep voice came from behind me.

I turned my head slowly to see what sort of nerd had just put his foot in his king-sized mouth. It was the jock from the basketball team—the sexy-eyed one whose name I didn't know.

He was a little taller than Andy, and his dark brown hair was much shorter than my brother's. Andy had let his grow long, and he pulled it back with an elastic band for comps. The way he did it, you'd have trouble knowing it wasn't just slicked back and short.

But I wasn't paying much attention to this guy's hair. It was his smile that fascinated me, and just about knocked me flat.

"I'm one of the teachers," I murmured, still watching the way his lips curved upward as he looked down at me.

Suddenly, his eyes turned dull, and the smile was gone. "You're kidding."

"No, I'm not." I smiled at him in spite of how irritating it always was when someone my own age cut down dancing. "My parents own this place. I'm helping my father with the class."

"Oh," was all he could get out.

We walked across the floor as my father started talking about how important it was at a wedding to be able to tell which dance the band or deejay was playing before you started dancing. I'd memorized his lecture and tuned him out.

"I'm Joe Ernst," the jock whispered.

"Carrie Clark."

He wasn't even trying to listen to my father. He kept staring at me. "I've seen you at school," he said, "during the week. But you never come to the games on Saturday."

"I don't have time. I have to practice, or else I'm working at the studio."

Joe nodded. "That's cool."

"Oh," I teased, "you don't think these lessons are *dumb* any more?"

His long face flushed pink. "Sorry."

My father's voice cut across the room. "Carrie, please come here."

I snapped out of my preoccupation with Joe and smiled at Dad as I strode across the room toward him.

"Carrie and I will demonstrate the difference between a waltz, a foxtrot, and the swing," he announced.

When the music ended and we'd finished our demonstration, the group clapped politely and I made a cheesy little curtsy. As I straightened up, I caught Joe's dark eyes. He was grinning at me, looking *very* interested.

I felt a tickle race up my spine, and wondered if he liked me. Just a little.

The rest of the lesson went pretty well, considering most of the students had to be told, "No, the other left foot," forty-two times. One man stepped on his fiancée's toe so hard she had to sit out the rest of the class. One woman jammed the heel of her shoe into another woman's instep when they collided. But all in all, it wasn't half bad. Some of them could even keep time with the music.

Because we'd rotated partners, I got to dance with Joe a few times, along with the other men. At the end of the class he came over to me.

"So, how'd I do?" he asked, flashing a smug smile.

"Not bad," I allowed.

"Not bad? Didn't you see me sweep that woman across the floor when we were waltzing?"

I laughed. "You looked more like you were dragging her in a wrestling grip." He looked disappointed. "Never mind," I added quickly. "You did fine for a beginner."

He puffed up, his pride restored. "My mom watches those ballroom dancers on the PBS channel. Now I can tell her there's nothing to it!"

I felt my skin prickle. He was beginning to get to me. "I don't know about—"

"Really," he insisted. "I bet anyone with decent coordination could do what they do."

I stopped in the middle of the room and stared at him. "Just like anyone with the least coordination could score thirty-two points in a game against Loyola?"

Joe grinned. "You've been following my scores!"

"A lucky guess," I corrected him. "You've got one enormous ego, you know that? One minute you're telling me you can do, after a single lesson, what it takes professionals years to learn. The next minute, you think I have nothing better to do than watch you throw balls through metal rings."

He laughed, thrusting his hands into his jeans pockets. "Well, at least I don't wear one of those starched penguin suits and tiptoe around like some ballet nerd."

I rolled my eyes. "You're only saying that because you have no idea how tough professional dancing can be. Dancers have to train hard, just as hard as athletes for any sport."

He chuckled. "Yeah, right."

"Forget it!" I snapped. Obviously, Joe was just like all the kids at school used to be, before they started asking me for new steps for hand dancing.

The crowd in the foyer was thinning out fast as people grabbed their coats and headed for home. The women looked flushed with excitement. The men looked relieved that the ordeal was over.

I dashed behind the desk and started marking down names as a new crop of students arrived for private lessons.

"Hey, see you next week," Joe said, as he slipped out the door.

I didn't look up at him, but I could imagine his smile. The smile that got me feeling all loose and breathless inside, but made me furious, too, because he was poking fun at what I most loved in all the world.

I couldn't figure out if I hated him or liked him— a lot.

5 `` But it won't happen again!'' I argued with my mother at closing time that same night. She shook her head. "I don't like the idea of your being here alone, Carrie, not after the burglary.''

"It wasn't a *real* burglary,'' I groaned. That sounded too dramatic for one of Miranda's pranks ... or something a bunch of neighborhood kids might have pulled. "Fifty bucks, some CDs, and one dress. You make it sound like a master criminal knocked off Donald Trump's penthouse!''

"You might have been here alone,'' she said tightly. "Desperate people do desperate things.''

"Dad?'' I begged.

"Why do you want to stay, Carrie?'' he asked. His voice sounded as tired as he looked. He obviously wanted to avoid an argument, which was to my advantage.

"It's hard for me to chill at home,'' I told him, trying to be at least a little honest. "Here it's quiet, and I can concentrate better on my homework. I won't stay long, I promise. Please.''

He looked at my mother. "We did have the locks changed."

She sighed and picked up her purse. "You can stay for an hour, then one of us will drive over to pick you up."

"But Mom—"

She gave me one of her that's-the-end-of-it looks. I shut my mouth, knowing anything else I might say would only make things worse.

The real reason I wanted to stay at the studio that night was Miranda. I knew she'd been working at her aunt's shop that afternoon, but Vivaldi's closed at 9:00 P.M. It was now almost 10:00, and when I'd lowered the blinds a few minutes earlier, I'd seen her white Honda Civic pull into the alley beside the shop.

She must have forgotten something, I reasoned. Since I wanted to talk to her alone, this seemed like the perfect opportunity.

I didn't know what I was going to say. I didn't feel like apologizing for blowing up at her in the hallway at school. She'd deserved that and more for a long time. But I supposed there was a slim chance she hadn't been the one to break in. If it hadn't been her, maybe she'd been around last night. Maybe she'd seen someone or something suspicious. And if she *had* stolen the dress, maybe there was a way I could convince her to give it back.

After everyone had left the studio, I stood at the window, peering through the plastic slats of the blinds at the row of shops across the street, working up my courage. A few people were walking along the sidewalk, out for a late cup of coffee and dessert at the pastry shop at the end of the block, or heading home after pizza and beer at Strapazzi's, which was always crowded.

There was no moon that night. It was darker than dark. And both of the streetlights nearest the alley where I'd seen Miranda's car disappear were out.

I focused on the brick front of Vivaldi's Collectibles. There were lights on in the first floor, but no sign of activity.

Suddenly a shadow flitted across one of the windows. Miranda, I guessed. My stomach flip-flopped nervously. I wasn't looking forward to confronting her.

Slowly, I gathered together my books and pulled on my jacket. I was determined to do what had to be done. One way or another, I wanted my gown back.

November in Maryland . . . some days the temperatures reached sixty degrees and felt almost spring-like. Other days, squirrels hustled around like little gray-suited businessmen, getting in those last few acorns—and you knew it was going to be a bitter winter.

Tonight the air felt damp and chilly, and I pulled the collar of my suede jacket up around my cheeks. Slinging my bookbag over my shoulder, I looked right then left before dashing across Allegheny Street. The shadow passed the window again, then, just as I was nearing the front door of the antique shop with its gilded lettering and shiny brass knocker, a second, differently shaped shadow appeared then faded.

''Now what?'' I muttered.

I lingered on the sidewalk, wondering what to do since Miranda obviously wasn't alone. Before I could make up my mind whether to knock on the door or go away, the light went out.

There were several explanations—she and whoever she'd brought with her were leaving for the night, or maybe she'd brought a boy along and what they were

33

doing didn't require a light. I smiled at that possibility. If it were a guy, I thought hopefully, I could snitch on her to Andy and he'd have to come to his senses. Then again, maybe her aunt had just stayed late.

With a frightening jolt, another thought occurred to me.

What if the same person who'd broken into the studio last night had just broken into the antique store? There was obviously a lot more valuable stuff there. What if the unspeakable things my mother's overactive imagination had imagined came true, but Miranda was the victim?

Without considering any more possibilities, I ran the last few steps toward Vivaldi's front door and banged hard with my fists.

"Miranda! Are you in there?"

There was no answer.

"Miranda, are you all right?" I pressed my ear to the door and listened, trying to still my ragged breathing so I could hear. But there was no sound from inside. All I could hear was my own heart whamming away in my chest.

I looked up and down the street. No one was in sight now.

Maybe she's left, I thought. Maybe I'd missed her pulling out of the alley. If the shadows were both those of intruders, there was no need to do anything but call the police. If her car was gone from the alley, I'd know.

I walked quickly to the mouth of the narrow passage between two buildings. Dimly, I could make out the shape of a white vehicle sitting near the back door of the antique store.

Damn, I thought. Now I had to do something.

Slowly, I entered the alley, trying to move without

making a sound. My mouth felt dry, and I sensed I was doing something stupid, but something made me go on. Every step I took, no matter how carefully, seemed to grate loud and long on the pavement.

It's probably none of my business, I kept telling myself. *She's probably got a boy in there with her, and they're doing something obscene like making out on top of a Louis XV desk.*

Then an even more disgusting thought crept into my head. What if the boy with her was Andy?

He'd kill me if I walked in on them. On the other hand, I'd never speak to him again if he and Miranda . . .

There was a noise off to my left, in the alley. It sounded like something shifting its weight, stealthily, behind a dumpster. I peered into the black shadows but could see nothing beyond the hulking shape of the huge, metal garbage bin.

"Is someone there?" I whispered hoarsely.

A soft shuffling sound came again. Closer.

I looked ahead to where Miranda's car was parked. Only ten feet from the passenger door was the entrance to the antique shop. I had no way of knowing whether or not it was unlocked. If someone was lurking in the alley, waiting to jump me, I'd be trapped if I ran for the door and it wouldn't open. I shot a quick look backwards, over my shoulder. The dim light from Allegheny Street beckoned to me.

Spinning around, I ran as hard as I could for the street. When I burst onto the sidewalk, I didn't stop there but crossed the street. As soon as my trembling hands could fit the key into the front door of the studio's office building, I let myself into the lobby and raced for the stairs.

It wasn't until I was on the second flight that I heard

35

the lobby door wheeze open, and realized I hadn't locked it behind me.

Bad move, I thought grimly.

Someone had followed me inside.

Fear prickled through my nerves as I ran up the steps and through the stairwell door. Fumbling with my keys, I searched clumsily for the familiar one that would open the studio door. *If I can lock myself inside*, I thought, *if I can just get inside and lock the door behind me, I'll call the police and . . .*

Then my eyes fell on the shiny new lock, and the bottom fell out of my stomach. Mom hadn't given me the new set of keys. I couldn't get back in. I was trapped.

Footsteps climbed the stairs toward me. Steps, moving cautiously upward. Heavy steps, trying to be quiet.

I let out an involuntary whimper. "No!"

Looking around frantically for another way out, I stared at the door of the only other office on the third floor. A consulting business of some kind. I didn't have a key for that door either. Other than the stairs, there was only the elevator, and it was so poky I doubted it would reach me before the person who had followed me into the building came through the stairwell door and cornered me.

I threw myself at the elevator button and jammed it down with my thumb—one, two, three, four times—then stood back, waiting breathlessly, counting the seconds as my mouth dried up. The steps on the stairs slowed, then stopped. The door inched slowly open.

"Come on, *come on*!" I whispered hoarsely at the elevator doors. "Open . . . *open*!"

I could hear the motor grinding away inside the wall, struggling to lift the little passenger box the last few inches. At the same moment as a figure stepped out of the stairwell, the elevator doors eased open. Without daring to look behind me, I threw myself between the metal sliders and banged the ground-floor button.

"Wait!" a voice shouted.

I pressed myself against the back wall of the elevator compartment, praying the doors would close. They did. Miraculously, the elevator started its snail-paced downward journey, creaking and groaning all the way.

As soon as it stopped at the bottom floor, I exploded through the doors. I was halfway across the lobby when someone tackled me from behind, dragging me by the waist, back into the shadows.

"Please don't!" I cried out.

A thousand violent images flashed through my mind. The stuff you see on TV crime shows that end in scenes with body bags and chalk outlines.

At first, the voice that shouted at me failed to penetrate my panic. Then I began to understand words.

Someone I knew was saying, "It's okay, Carrie. Calm down. I just wanted to catch you before you left for the night."

The arm around my waist loosened. I pushed free and jerked around to face . . .

"Joe!" I grinned deliriously at him, then recovered and slugged him in the arm. His muscle hurt my fist. "What are you doing here? You scared me to death!"

He laughed self-consciously. "Sorry. I left my jacket upstairs. I came back to get it."

"Your *jacket*!" I shouted. "You chased me up three flights of stairs and down again for a jacket?"

"It's leather. Those things walk if you don't keep an eye on them."

I groaned, shaking my head at him. "Well, no one can get it tonight. My dad had the locks changed today and forgot to give me the new keys. We're locked out along with any would-be jacket thieves."

He shut his eyes for a moment in frustration. Only then, when their light was shut off, did I realize what a deep blue they were. I found myself gazing a little too blissfully into them when they opened again.

"Look," I said quickly, "I'll tell my dad to put your coat in his office when he opens up tomorrow. It'll be safe there."

Joe nodded, apparently satisfied. "Okay. Walk you home?"

I thought for a moment. "I was supposed to wait for my mom or dad to pick me up, but now I don't feel like staying." I glanced nervously toward the antique store's windows, which were still dark. There was still the question of Miranda and whoever was in there with her . . . and whoever or whatever had chased me out of the alley.

"Where's the nearest pay phone?" I asked.

"Why?"

"I want to bake a cake, what do you think?"

Joe looked sheepish. "Down the block, I think. In front of the drug store."

I pushed through the lobby door, remembering to lock it after Joe had followed me out. We walked briskly down the sidewalk.

"You look upset. You aren't still mad at me, are you?"

"No." I stopped and turned to look back at Vivaldi's. "Something strange happened just before you showed up." I told him about the shadows in the window, then the sounds in the alley that had spooked me.

"Well, neither one was me," he said. "I was down the street in front of Strapazzi's when I spotted you tearing across the street toward the studio."

"Did you see anyone following me?"

"No."

I sighed. So whoever had chased me out of the alley had stopped at Allegheny Street. And that was when Joe took off after me.

"You're afraid someone might have broken into the antique store?" he guessed.

"Yeah. And Miranda's car is still parked in the alley, which means she's up there." I bit down on my lip. "I think I'd better at least call and make sure everything's okay, you know, after what happened at the studio."

"I heard about that," Joe said. He led me to the pay phone and held out a quarter.

"Thanks." I punched in the number at Vivaldi's. I have a photographic memory for numbers; it's a weird trick I picked up from memorizing dance sequences. The phone number and address of every store and restaurant on the entire street is indelibly etched in my brain.

The phone rang, then rang again and again.

"What's happening?" Joe whispered.

"No answer yet."

He nodded, then I felt him stiffen beside me. "Look."

I followed his glance. The white car was pulling out of the alley between Vivaldi's and the travel agency next door. "That's Miranda's car."

"Well, I guess she must be okay," he said.

I listened for three more rings, then hung up. "Guess so," I muttered, trying to see through the windshield as the Civic whipped past us. I especially wanted to see who was in the passenger seat. If it was Andy, he'd have some questions to answer—like, what kind of dance steps do you practice in the dark, dear brother?

I couldn't make out any faces.

Whoever was in the car with Miranda, it hadn't been Andy. He was already home when I got there. I could hear one of his CDs blasting away behind the closed door of his bedroom.

I decided not to mention Miranda or the shadows in Vivaldi's window. If I told him now, without having any proof she'd been up there with another guy, he wouldn't believe me. He'd think I'd made it up to get him to come back with me.

Anyway, if Miranda had another boyfriend, Andy would find out soon enough. She wasn't exactly the subtle type, and news like that travels fast around Mencken High.

The next morning Andy drove to school, so I hitched a ride with him. Neither of us was totally awake, so we didn't talk much on the way.

Diana and Tammy were standing at the edge of the parking lot when we pulled in. They started running toward the car before Andy had a chance to set the parking brake.

As soon as I opened my door, Diana reached in and yanked me out of the seat. "Did you hear yet?" she screamed in my face.

I'd never seen her so agitated. Of the three of us, she was always the calm one.

"Hear what?" I looked at Tammy, who seemed comatose by comparison. She was chomping in a relaxed way on a cherry Tastycake, but I knew that meant she was worried about something. She either starved herself or binged when something was bothering her.

"Did you hear about Miranda?" Diana gasped, hugging her books to her chest like a shield.

"What about her?" Andy shouted over the roof of the car.

Diana stared at him, her eyes enormous brown pools. "She's dead."

I looked at her, understanding about as much of what she'd said as I did of the Pythagorean Theorem.

Andy came up beside me. "What are you talking about?" he demanded, sounding angry.

"I-I said, she's dead," Diana whispered.

"The police are in the principal's office right now," Tammy explained, balling up her Tastycake wrapper and pushing it into her coat pocket. "The Hemingways live two doors down from us. Around three o'clock this morning the police showed up at their house, and my mom called Miranda's mom a couple of hours later to see if everything was all right. It wasn't."

"Oh no . . ." I breathed. A thousand thoughts raced through my mind, but I couldn't sort them out at that moment. "Do you know what happened?"

Tammy produced another Tastycake from her coat pocket and began unwrapping it. Vanilla cream, this time.

"Apparently, Miranda's parents got worried when she didn't come home last night by midnight, like she said she would. She told them she was studying with friends. But when they called around, she wasn't with any of them. Then they called the police."

I shook my head. "Her car was at the antique gallery close to eleven o'clock."

"Well, who knows with Miranda," Diana said.

"She might have told her parents anything, if she didn't want them to know where she was." Diana didn't like Miranda any more than I did—mostly, I thought, because of me. Diana was a loyal friend. If someone was mean to me or Tammy, she'd have nothing to do with them.

Tammy's mouth hung open, halfway to her cake. "You were *there*?"

"Not at Vivaldi's. I was at the studio." My mind was whirring, trying to retrieve details from last night. The shadows . . . the Civic . . . the predatory sounds in the alley . . .

"Did you see anything suspicious while you were there?" Andy asked.

I'd forgotten he was with us, listening to all of this. I looked at him for the first time since Diana had delivered her shocking news. His face was white, and his lips were pressed together and an awful shade of blue.

"Yeah. A lot," I admitted dismally. "I saw someone—two people in the front windows. Then the lights went out."

Diana shivered. "Creepy."

I continued. "Miranda's car was parked in the alley, so I figured she was there."

Tammy polished off Tastycake #2. "My mom said the police found her car parked a couple of blocks away from the store."

Had someone left the studio with her, then killed her in the car? I was confused. "Where was . . . you know, the body?" I stammered. My stomach heaved at the last word, and I hoped with all my heart that what I already guessed wasn't true.

"In Vivaldi's," Diana said solemnly. "She'd been smashed over the head with something."

42

Now I really felt as if I was going to be sick. The horrible truth was, I might have been able to help Miranda if I'd gone into Vivaldi's instead of running away. I'd watched her killer drive away in her car.

"I'd better go talk to the police," I whispered.

6

In a way, the police found me before I found them.

I was headed for Principal Forest's office when the first bell rang. I would have ignored it under the circumstances, except I saw a man and a woman in Baltimore County police uniform walk into my homeroom.

They were both carrying notepads and wearing guns. I figured they weren't there to get pointers on algebra from Mrs. Chavez.

The man was short, with black hair that looked waxy and too thick to be real. His toupee clung around the sides of his face like the legs of a hairy spider. He also had very bad skin.

The woman was big, both tall and wide, and moved awkwardly between the close rows of desks. But she wasn't really fat, just strong looking. She had red hair, chopped off in a no-nonsense cut just below her earlobes. and huge hands that almost concealed the purse-sized notebook she carried. Andy would have called her *one scary broad.*

When I took my seat, the two cops were talking with Mrs. Chavez at the back of the room. She was nodding at everything they said. I'd never seen her in such an agreeable mood, but she wasn't smiling.

A minute later she strode to the front of the room with purpose. "Class, Officers Landry and Drake wish to have a word with you."

I'd never been in a classroom as quiet as this one was now. The funny thing was, by now everyone probably knew why the police had come, but the cops thought they were breaking tragic news.

Landry, the redhead, leaned backward against the edge of Mrs. Chavez's desk and surveyed every face in the room. "A few of you may have already heard some troubling rumors this morning."

I looked around. As I'd expected, I didn't see one puzzled expression.

"A girl from this class, Miranda Hemingway, died last night. We have reason to believe that she was murdered." I had to give her points for dramatic impact; she knew when to pause for the right effect. Students responded with gasps and whispered comments.

Red continued, "We need all the help we can get to find the person or people responsible. Baltimore County police and Miranda's parents hope we can count on your help."

She paused again, this time to look around the room. No one said a word. I swallowed. Boy, was I going to give them an earful.

"Sergeant Drake and I will be talking with each of you, and all of the students in Miranda's other classes. It will help if you let us know about particular friends Miranda might have had, or people she didn't get along with. And if any of you saw Miranda yesterday, any time after school, you should let us know that too."

They retreated to the long table at the rear of the

room, and started calling people back one at a time. Mrs. Chavez gave us busy work, algebra exercises on ditto sheets.

My seat was in the last row. I couldn't help listening in as the cops questioned the first few people.

Most of the kids had known Miranda. She was sort of hard not to know because she was always making a big deal about everything she did. She dressed to be noticed, she talked loudly, and when she moved across a room, she did it with the kind of drama that attracted attention.

She was like that on a dance floor too. You just *had* to look at her. That was good for catching a judge's eye, but bad if you happened to blow steps, like Miranda often did.

Diana turned and glanced over her shoulder at me, her expression solemn. I wondered what she was thinking. Tammy and Andy were in other homerooms. They'd get their chances to talk about Miranda later.

I tried to work on the math, but I couldn't tune out the cops' questions, the same ones over and over.

"How well did you know Miranda Hemingway?"

"Where were you last night, between the hours of 9:00 P.M. and 2:00 A.M.?"

"Did you *like* Miranda?"

"Do you know of anyone who would want to hurt her?"

Try half the school, I thought irreverently, then was sorry I'd let my brain stoop that low. She might have been selfish, nasty, and devious, but she didn't deserve to get her skull crushed and die when she was only seventeen.

"Isabelle Vane," I heard Red call out.

I turned my head just enough to catch a glimpse of a girl I usually saw only in homeroom. She looked even more like a scared mouse than normal. Her eyes were huge and lusterless, and her hands knotted and unknotted on the table as she spoke.

Her answers were the same as a lot of kids'. "Yes I knew her . . . no, not really a friend . . . of course I don't know who'd want to hurt her."

I did another problem, letting the numbers fit themselves together automatically.

There was a pause, then Isabelle's voice returned, sounding stronger.

"I'm taking a lot of art classes. I'd sign up for all art, and nothing else, if I could. I'm sort of okay at stuff like that, better than English and math . . ."

Isabelle, you just don't know how to sell yourself, I thought. Although I didn't know her well, I'd seen some of her paintings and original jewelry designs displayed at the annual Towsontowne Craft and Art Festival. She had her own booth, just like the professional artists who'd driven down from Pennsylvania and New York. Isabelle was really talented. But she was still a mouse, unable to let on she was any good.

I glanced back at the faces of the two cops. They were looking at her in a patronizing way, as if she were telling them about her crayon drawings of Mickey Mouse.

They called two more people to their table. We were going up and down the rows. They'd almost reached me when the door opened and in walked Joe. He went right to them.

This time I put down my pencil and listened hard.

"I heard you were in here," he said nervously. "I was there last night, right outside the antique store." He lowered his voice so that I had to strain to hear him. "I got to Allegheny Street the first time about 7:00 P.M.," he explained, then went on to tell them

47

about the dance lesson, and going back later in the evening for his jacket.

"And did you get it?" Toup asked, scratching at a few out-of-place hairs in front of his ear.

"No. The studio was locked. I met the girl whose parents own the dance studio, out front, but she couldn't get back in."

That's not all that happened, I thought, frowning at the sheet of paper in front of me. I wondered why he didn't tell them the rest, about our chase up and down the stairs.

"Did you go inside Vivaldi's?" Toup asked.

"I was across the street from it. No, I didn't go inside," Joe said.

I glanced back at them and saw Red watching Joe intently. She asked. "Did you see anything suspicious?"

"Not at first," Joe said slowly. "But then we— that's me and Carrie Clark, the girl I was telling you about—well, we saw Miranda's car pull out of the alley."

"And you thought that was suspicious?"

"Not really, not then at least. But this morning, after I heard what had happened to her last night . . . well, it must not have been her driving the car. Maybe she was already dead by then." He stared at his hands.

Their discussion went on for another ten minutes, the cops writing furiously, taking down every word he said. Joe was their gold mine, so far. They released him, telling him to call them if he remembered anything else. He left the room without even looking at me.

Red skipped over the next three people in my row and called my name next. I walked back to the table, feeling sick to my stomach.

It wasn't that I didn't want to help them find Miranda's killer, I really did. But I was afraid they'd think I'd been stupid for not calling the police or Miranda's aunt to report the strange shadows. And what about the "thing" in the alley that had chased me? A dozen maybe-I-should-haves rattled around in my brain, weighing me down.

I sat in the chair every other student had taken and looked at Red. Before she could ask a question I said, "I was right outside Vivaldi's when she was killed."

The cops exchanged glances then looked at me.

"Why do you say that?" Red asked. "Your friend told us the two of you were in the street, but how do you know that was when she was murdered?"

"It has to have been, because I saw Miranda's car pull into the alley around 10:00 P.M., when I was lowering the blinds in my parents' studio."

"You're the one who was there the night before, when someone tried to break into the studio?" Toup asked.

"Yes," I said, surprised that they'd made the connection.

Red leaned forward and studied my face. "We heard about that—mostly dancing stuff missing. You were brave to stay late another night," she said thoughtfully. It wasn't a question, but it wasn't exactly a statement of fact. She sounded as if she was thinking the words over, and all the secret, inner meanings they might have.

"I'm not brave," I said. "I just didn't want to go home yet, and the locks had been changed, so I wasn't worried about—"

"You're having problems at home?" Red interrupted sympathetically.

"No, we're not having *problems*," I said. She was

getting a little off the track. "I just wanted to stay a while, by myself."

Toup scratched his wigline again. "Were you waiting for your boyfriend to show up?"

"My boyfriend?" I sputtered.

"Yes," he said, glancing at his notes. "Joseph Ernst."

I rolled my eyes before I remembered how much adults hated that. "He's not my boyfriend. We're not even friends. He just signed up for one of the beginner classes, and he left his jacket behind. He wanted me to let him back in, but I didn't have the new keys."

The cops nodded in synchronized motion—like those goofy dolls with their heads on springs that people used to put in the backs of cars.

"Look, it's very important, what I saw," I said. "Can we get to the major stuff? Like the shadows and the person in the alley and—"

"Person in the alley?" Red's eyes narrowed.

"Yes. You see, I was coming out of the studio and I crossed the street. I'd seen a shadow in the front window of Vivaldi's, so I figured Miranda was still there and I wanted to talk to her. Then, as I was crossing the street, I saw another shadow."

"Possibly hers again?" asked Toup.

"No, this one seemed bigger."

"And then what?" the woman prompted.

I thought for a moment, trying to get the order of events straight in my head. I didn't want to make a mistake. "Well, I figured Miranda might have brought along a friend, and that was cool. But on second thought I decided I'd better check things out, since someone had already broken into the dance studio. I knocked on the front door, but no one answered."

"And then?"

"Well, I knocked again and waited for a while, but there was still no answer, so I went around to the alley to see if her car was still there."

"Why wouldn't you just assume she'd left by that hour?" Toup asked.

"If she'd left, then someone was in there who shouldn't have been. If her car wasn't in the alley, I was going to call the police. If it was still there, I'd try to get inside and make sure she was all right."

Red breathed in and out in shallow breaths, looking a little too excited by what I was saying. "Was the car there? What about this person in the alley?"

"The car was there—her white Civic. And someone was hiding behind the dumpster. I could hear him moving."

"You saw no one?"

"No, but he was there, I'm sure. I heard him, then he chased me as far as the street."

"Probably a cat." Toup chuckled. "Damn strays are everywhere these days."

Red ignored him. "You didn't turn and look, even for a second?" she asked.

"No," I said, "I was too busy running."

They both wrote something down, then looked at each other, and, finally, turned to me.

"That's all," I said.

I could tell them about being so spooked I'd tried to run back to the studio for protection, but Joe had left that out so he probably thought it was unimportant. Besides, there seemed to be no point confusing the situation.

"Why didn't you call the police when you and your friend saw Miranda's car pull out of the alley?" Red asked.

She looked me in the eyes. I had to turn away. Her

gaze was so intense, it made me nervous.

"I-I didn't think there was any reason to call then."

"Being chased down a dark alley and suspecting someone has broken into a store seems enough," Toup commented casually.

I looked at him; he didn't have Red's laser eyes. "But by then I didn't think anyone had broken in. When I saw Miranda's car leave, I thought she'd had a friend upstairs with her, and she and her friend had left. I didn't want to start trouble for her."

"You liked her, then?" Red asked, watching my face the way a cat watches the hole into which a mouse has just disappeared.

I drew my tongue between my lips. Maybe they'd make me take a lie-detector test. "No," I admitted, "I didn't like her. She was mean and selfish."

Red flipped back a few pages in her notebook. "You two were competitors, opponents in the dance world."

Her question hit me out of the blue. She'd *known* about Miranda and me, about us dancing and probably about our hating each other's guts. Yet she hadn't let on the whole time. I wondered who had told her.

"Yes, we competed against each other. And it wasn't a very friendly competition," I added, then anticipated her next question. "I wouldn't have wanted anything like this to happen to her, though. And I *didn't* kill her."

She smiled, but no humor showed in her eyes. "Even though she stole your partner?"

Good grief! I thought. *How did she find all this out so fast?*

"My brother had told me he was going to dance with her. I was ticked off at him, but—" I shook my head. "It's sick to even think of someone killing an-

52

other person over a dance competition."

"People have intentionally injured or plotted to kill champion tennis players and Olympic figure skaters," Toup pointed out. "Why not dancers?"

I shook my head. I could feel sweat pooling under my sweater; my hands were shaking. "All I can tell you is, it wasn't me."

Sometime during our conversation the bell for first period must have rung, because the room was now empty, except for us. I hadn't even noticed until that minute.

The two cops exchanged coplike looks and leaned back in their chairs.

"If you think I killed Miranda Hemingway," I said shakily, "shouldn't I have a lawyer sitting here with me?"

That's the way it always worked on TV detective shows. The cops had to read you your rights and inform you that you had the right to a lawyer.

Red lifted her lips in a tight smile. "No one's accusing you of anything," she said. "We're just giving you an opportunity to get anything off your chest that might be bothering you."

"Anything that might give us more information about what happened last night, about how Miranda Hemingway died," Toup added.

"There were two shadows in the window," I repeated like a neurotic parrot. "Someone chased me out of the alley, and a few minutes later, I saw Miranda's car leave. I never saw the face of the driver, and I don't know if anyone else was in the car. That's all I can tell you."

7

"**I can't stop thinking** about what that woman cop said," I told Diana at lunchtime in the cafeteria, and shivered at the thought.

"What's that?"

"She said, 'We're giving you the opportunity to get anything off you chest that might be bothering you.'"

"So?" Tammy shrugged and halfheartedly shoved a spoonful of yogurt into her mouth. After a morning of pigging out, she was now on one of her instant diets. "That sounds like they're just trying to be nice."

I shook my head. "No. It sounds like they've already made up their minds that I had something to do with Miranda's death."

"Why would you do a thing like that?" Diana asked, avoiding my eyes, as if she already knew.

"To get my brother back as a dance partner and put Miranda out of the running. Permanently."

Tammy studied me thoughtfully over the lip of her strawberry-banana yogurt cup. "They don't have any proof you did anything. Do they?"

"Of course not!" It almost sounded like she was on the cops' side: "I didn't *do* anything! But I don't

54

have an alibi either. I was alone in the studio, then I crossed the street to the antique shop, but there's no one who can say I didn't actually go inside.''

Tammy licked her spoon. "You know, Miranda was pretty awful to a lot of kids. Some people might think she deserved to die. I'll bet no one would really blame you if—"

"Don't even *think* that!" I hissed at her. "I couldn't kill anyone, you know that.''

She blinked at me, dropping her plastic spoon into the empty cup. "I know you wouldn't hurt anyone *intentionally*. But what if Miranda said something really obnoxious, and you just sort of . . . sort of lost it, like in the hall the other day?''

I turned to Diana for support. But I could see the same uncertainty in her eyes.

"If I'd killed her accidentally, I'd say so. I wouldn't make up a bunch of lies." I thought for a moment. "Besides, if I murdered Miranda, who was driving her car? Remember, Joe Ernst saw her Civic leave the alley, too.''

Diana rolled her eyes. "Joe is hot for you. He'd say anything.''

"Where'd you hear that?" I shouted, then remembered where we were and lowered my voice. Kids at the next table were looking at us and whispering. "Never mind," I said. "The fact is, someone drove off in Miranda's car after she was dead. Joe didn't make that up.''

"Say I'm the police," Tammy said. "I might think Joe drove it away himself, to help you out, then made up the story about watching someone else drive it off. No one saw the two of you together, right? You could have just walked home and told your parents Joe had walked you home, while he was ditching the car. They'd never know.''

"Or," Diana added, her voice rising dramatically, "it could have been *Andy* in the car."

"Andy?" I choked out.

"Sure, why not? He's your brother. He's stuck by you all these years, through all those competitions." Diana seemed to warm to her task of creating a murder story. "Maybe he realized he'd gone too far by ditching you for Miranda, so he went to the studio to tell you he was sorry. But when he got there, you'd already conked sweet Miranda on the head, and all he could do was help you get rid of evidence and make it look like someone else killed her."

I stared hopelessly at the two of them. "Thanks for the vote of confidence, you guys."

"You have to admit these are logical possibilities," Diana protested.

"No, they're not!" I stood up from my seat at the table, and collided with something.

A dull "UMPH!" came from close by. I spun around.

Isabelle Vane sat on the floor with a slice of pizza in her lap and a pool of soda all around her. Her plump legs stuck out from her skirt as she struggled to get to her feet.

"I'm sorry!" I told her, trying to help her up.

"It's okay," she mumbled, looking at the ruined pizza on the floor. "I wasn't very hungry."

"Your skirt is all wet." I pointed to the dark, Coke-stained circle where she'd been sitting.

"Oh," she said, looking embarrassed.

"Come on." I tossed Diana and Tammy an irritated look. "Let's go to the girls' room. I'll help you dry off."

56

"Don't be mad!" Diana called out after us. "We're just trying to help by telling you what the police will be thinking."

I'd already figured that out. The police would look first for motive. Mine was the most obvious one. But Andy was my brother and he might do something desperate for me, even if Miranda were his new partner. And Joe? What was he? Not my boyfriend. He wasn't really connected with me in any way except that his mother had signed him up for dance lessons. But I could see why the police might think there was something between us.

Isabelle was muttering something about not needing any help, when I looked at her out of my thoughts. Her tan wool skirt was dripping with dark brown liquid. She was always so neatly dressed, a preppie dinosaur in the middle of a school full of rumpled jeans and oversized flannel shirts. Grunge was *in* at Mencken High.

She looked terribly embarrassed.

"I saw the police interviewing you this morning," I said, as we pushed through the cafeteria doors, heading toward the girls' room. "I didn't realize you even knew Miranda."

Isabelle brushed straight, mocha-colored strands of hair from her eyes and over her shoulder. "We met in madrigal choir. I helped her study a few times," she admitted stiffly, as if she didn't want to get involved.

I couldn't blame her.

We reached the girls' room. I pulled a fistful of paper towels out of the dispenser and dampened them with water from the faucet.

"The skirt's already wet enough," Isabelle protested.

"This is to dilute the Coke. Cold water will help take out the stain so it won't set." I looked up at her from where I was squatting on the floor. "You must have ways to thin your paints or even remove them if you make a mistake while you're working on a painting," I pointed out.

She looked puzzled for a moment, as if she hadn't heard me at first, then shrugged. "Oh sure. Right."

"Turn around," I said. "I'll get the back, then we'll dry you off the best we can."

She stood silently while I worked on her skirt. I'd had a lot experience dealing with emergency stains in costumes. Twice, Miranda—at least I was pretty sure it had been her—had sabotaged my outfits. I'd been furious at the time. Now it just seemed like a dumb trick. Dying was a lot worse.

"Do you know anyone who might have had a reason to kill Miranda?" I asked impulsively.

"Kill her?" Isabelle repeated. "No."

"Did you like her?"

"We got along okay, I guess," she said.

"Where did you two study?" I asked.

She gave me a funny look.

"I never saw the two of you together in school, or at the library."

She twisted her thick body around to check out the back of her skirt. "We studied at her aunt's antique shop or at my house."

I squeezed the wool of her skirt between fresh layers of paper towels, soaking up the moisture. "Were you at Vivaldi's last night?"

Isabelle pulled away. "Why would you ask me something like that?"

"Because I saw two people, two shadows really, in

the upstairs window. One could have been Miranda, the other might have been—"

"I wasn't there," she said quickly. "I was working on my art project in my parents' garage."

I nodded. "I wasn't accusing you of anything," I said, borrowing a line from the police. "I just thought you might have seen someone come into Vivaldi's as you left."

Isabelle's expression cleared. "I wish I had been there." She shook her head sadly. "Maybe Miranda would be alive now."

"It's not your fault you weren't," I said. Maybe she thought her size would intimidate a burglar. She was almost as big as Red. "If you *had* been there," I added, "maybe there would have been two bodies this morning."

"I suppose you're right," Isabelle said with a shudder. She smoothed her hands down the back of her skirt and smiled shyly at me. "Hey, it feels almost dry. Is the stain gone?"

"Most of it," I told her. "If you take it to the dry cleaner's this afternoon, they should be able to get the rest of it out."

Isabelle smiled again. "Thanks. I'm sorry I yelled at you about the questions. I guess this is pretty upsetting for everyone." She looked at me thoughtfully. "I heard about the break in at your parents' dance studio. I'm sorry your stuff got taken."

I nodded. "Maybe it will turn up. If the police find out who took my dress, maybe it will lead them to Miranda's killer."

"I hope so," Isabelle said.

"So, what do you say? Are you coming back to partner me for the Mid-Atlantics?" I asked Andy.

He'd agreed to drive me back to school that night, to pick up a notebook I'd forgotten and needed for homework.

"I don't know," he said slowly.

I stared at him across the front seat of the car. "Why not? Miranda's—"

"—out of the way?" he finished the sentence for me, but not the way I would have. His voice sounded brittle and angry.

"*You* don't think I killed her, do you?" I asked, shocked.

"I don't know what to think." He sighed. "Look, I know my sister's no murderer. But Miranda and I . . ."

"You had a thing for her, didn't you?" I asked, suddenly understanding how upset he was, and why.

"I don't know." He sounded less angry, just sad. "She was really determined to win, and she was so pretty. There was something about her that I . . . I just liked a lot."

I stared at his profile. It hadn't occurred to me that he'd be this broken up about her death.

"So, you don't want to dance with me ever again?" I asked.

"I didn't say that. It's just not something I can do now, because of the police."

I didn't understand. "Why not?"

He pulled up in front of the school. There were adult continuing ed classes, so the doors were still unlocked, even though it was almost 8:00 P.M.

"You said they might suspect you of killing her. Well," he explained, "if I go back to dancing with you, that will make things worse. It will look as if you got what you wanted. I was going to dance with

60

Miranda, you killed her, and I came back to be your partner.''

"I see," I murmured. There was a sick kind of logic in his reasoning. But there was something else he wasn't saying . . . something I couldn't quite put my finger on at first. Then it came to me, in parts and shadows. Andy was wondering if I could have killed Miranda. My own brother didn't believe me. "I'd better get my stuff," I said and quickly swung out of the car door.

I ran through the halls, trying not to think about the ugly thoughts that had rushed into my head a moment earlier. When I reached my locker, the entire wing was dark. I looked around for the light switch but couldn't find it.

I began to work on the combination, barely able to see the little hatch marks on the dial in the dim red light from the Exit sign. My locker was an upper, and I had to reach above my head to open it. A soft sound nearby interrupted me. I turned and waited, expecting to see the janitor, but no one came around the corner. I started over on the combination.

At last, I pulled open the locker door. Something that felt like heavy cobwebs spilled out on top of me, and an object clattered noisily to the tile floor.

"Help!" I screamed, trying to run backward while flailing with my arms at the mysterious net that had dropped over my head and arms. Tripping over my own feet, I fell on my backside.

"Help!" I shouted again. "Someone help me!"

I wrestled on the floor with whatever had leapt out of the locker at me. Finally, I got a grasp on it and pulled the wispy mass away from my face.

Andy ran up to me, looking as out of breath as I

felt. "I came in for a drink of water and heard you screaming! What's going on?"

"It *attacked* me," I said, pointing at the heap on the floor beside me.

Andy ran back to the hallway junction and flipped a switch while I scooted away from the *thing* on my hands and knees. The whole wing lit up brilliantly. I blinked, forcing my eyes to adjust to the glare. There, on the floor, mussed and shredded, was the creature that had assaulted me.

"Your peach gown," Andy said dryly.

I breathed in and out, in and out, trying to calm my hammering heart. My *stolen* gown. "It was jammed into my locker." I reached down and picked up two CD cases. "The missing music. Someone put all of this in my locker."

Andy looked at me. "Are you sure?"

A sudden chill passed through my bones. "What do you mean, am I sure? You see them here in front of us!"

He looked suddenly troubled. "Well, who else has your locker combination?"

"I don't know, a lot of my friends ... Diana, Tammy, you, others."

He took a deep breath. "Carrie, have you been straight with me? With the cops?"

"What are you talking about?" I huffed, reaching down to pick up my gown and shake it out. It really was a mess, all wrinkled, and some of the underskirts had torn when I'd fought with them.

"I mean," he said, "I know how much winning has always meant to you. I just don't know how far you'd go to win."

My mouth clunked open and I glared at him. "You don't really think I killed her, do you?"

62

"I told you, I'm not sure what to think," he said. "Maybe you figured by faking a break in at the studio, you could blame Miranda for your missing gown. It's the kind of stunt she might have played on you. Maybe you just wanted to get back at her, but the police didn't follow up on it and Miranda and you ended up arguing and . . . well, one thing led to another."

I couldn't answer him. My own brother suspected me of murder! With friends and family like this, I thought, who needs prosecuting attorneys?

"Carrie," he said gently, "if it happened that way, if it was an accident, it would be better to just tell the police. I've heard of cases like that. The person usually gets off pretty light."

"I can't believe you're saying this!"

"Carrie—"

"No!" I shouted at him. "I might just as well accuse *you* of killing her."

"She wasn't my rival," he said blankly.

"Sure, she was. You and I were partners, remember? Maybe you just pretended to like her, and you faked wanting to dance with her. Maybe that was just a way to get close to her, so you could—"

"Stop it, Carrie," he muttered. "You're hysterical."

I started crying, crying hard. If my own brother didn't believe me, how could I expect anyone else to?

"No!" I shouted.

I gathered up the pile of netting and lace and organdy in front of my stomach, like a fat woman trying to hug herself. Thoughts that had first struck me that afternoon and I'd started to tell Andy about a minute ago seemed even clearer—and just as terrifying.

"It might just as easily be you, Andy," I repeated between sobs. "It really might be."

"How? How?" he demanded, slamming my locker door shut and running after me. "I was home all night, studying."

"You *said* you were in your room," I pointed out, "but no one saw you. Your door was locked, and your CD player was switching itself, I could hear it from my room. For all Mom and Dad and I knew, you could have slipped out your window and gone to meet Miranda."

"You're being ridiculous," he groaned.

"No more ridiculous than you are when you say I might have killed her."

I threw the gown into the back seat of his car and collapsed into the passenger seat. He ran around to the other side and got in.

Andy drove without talking for five minutes, and I practiced deep breathing exercises, trying to calm down while I wiped the tears from my eyes. My mascara left sooty trails across the backs of my hands.

"I suppose the police already took fingerprints in Vivaldi's," I murmured.

Andy glanced at me, and frowned. "Yeah."

I could tell what his next question would be. "They won't find any of mine," I said. "I wasn't inside." I hesitated. "What about you?"

He watched the road as though he were afraid it would disappear if he looked away. "I was there plenty of times to see Miranda. They'll find mine."

I nodded and felt even worse. In a way, Miranda had won. She'd torn us apart by making us suspect each other of killing her.

I knew I couldn't just keep quiet about the gown showing up. Andy would tell Mom and Dad, and my parents would tell the police. Then it would look as if I'd been hiding something or, even worse, as if I'd made up the whole thing about the break in.

But, in a weird way, I felt as if by going to the cops I'd be doing exactly what the person who'd put the gown in my locker wanted me to do. I was almost sure I was walking into some sort of trap, yet I couldn't do anything but keep on walking into it until I discovered the truth. It was like having a bad dream, one you've had dozens of times before, so that you know something awful is going to happen any moment . . . but you can't stop it from happening.

I spent the rest of the day wondering how to tell Red and Toup the gown had shown up, without sounding like a liar or some dippy teenager who'd forgotten she'd left her dress in her locker. At last, I called the police station and left a message that I needed to talk to Officer Landry or Drake.

As soon as I hung up the phone in my dad's office, I heard Joe's voice in the foyer, talking to my mother.

We were having another Wedding Survival class to-night.

My father was teaching the foxtrot that night. It's a weird name for the easy, four-count dance older people do to ninety-eight percent of everything sung by Frank Sinatra or Tony Bennett. Personally, I prefer Gloria Estefan to Frank, but Tony's okay. His MTV bit was cool.

The class went well, I guess. I wasn't really thinking about what was going on. I just danced the steps, demonstrating each one with my father, then taking turns with the men in the class.

"You look like you're on another planet," Joe commented when I came to him.

"I wish I were," I muttered.

"What happened?"

I told him about the gown and CDs showing up in my locker. I didn't tell him about my conspiracy theory. He was enough of a tease without being fed ammunition.

"That's spooky," Joe said, watching his feet as he picked up each one then put it down, almost in time to the music. "It's like someone is trying to make you look bad."

"Exactly," I said. "Don't look at your feet."

"Why can't I?"

"It looks dumb."

"Where should I look while I'm dancing?" he asked, sounding frustrated.

"At your partner. And smile, you're supposed to be enjoying yourself."

"I'm not a very good actor," he grumbled.

We danced a few more bars, then he asked, "You want to go out for a pizza later? I'm meeting some of the guys from the team at Strapazzi's."

"I don't feel much like eating," I said apologetically.

He shrugged, stared at this feet, then remembered to keep his head up and pasted a forced smile on his face. "Did I tell you that taking dance lessons was my mother's idea?"

"At least eight times," I said. "Slow, slow, quick, quick. Slow, slow, quick, quick—that's it."

"I feel like a nerd." He looked down at his feet again.

I pinched his biceps.

"Ouch!" He glared at me.

"That's better, now dance and quit complaining," I ordered, trying not to laugh.

We switched partners again. By the time the hour was almost over, Joe was doing a lot better. Now he could turn a corner while doing his slow-slow-quick-quick, instead of just heading blindly into the mirrors.

"This is a really dumb dance," he muttered.

I gave him a dirty look. "I took first place in International foxtrot the last competition I entered."

"I'm not surprised," he said. "There's nothing to it."

"You've only learned two bronze-level steps. Wait until you get to the silver and gold stuff."

He laughed. "Hey, I promised my mother I'd take four weeks of this crap. Then I'm outta here."

I looked at him skeptically. "I bet I know why you're always making fun of dancing."

"Why?"

"You're afraid of what your buddies on the basketball team will think of you. I'll bet you didn't tell them you were coming here."

His back stiffened and his eyes darkened. "I don't care what anyone thinks. I do what I want to do."

"Do they know?"

"It doesn't matter."

"Do they *know*?" I repeated.

"No." He looked irritated.

I smiled. *One for my side*, I thought.

Five minutes before class time was up, my father told everyone to form a circle around the outside of the room. All the students obediently stepped back and put on listening faces.

"I know it's hard to imagine what a dance should look like if you've never seen it done properly . . ." he began.

I cringed, knowing what was coming. Any other time I wouldn't have minded showing off, but the idea that Joe was watching made me nervous.

"So," Dad continued, "Carrie and I will demonstrate a few of the more advanced steps you can look forward to learning." He held out his left hand to me and smiled.

You might think that dancing with your father would be pretty yucky, but you've never danced with *my* father. You could have three left feet, and he'd make you look like the Cinderella in the Disney cartoon, floating across the floor.

He and Mom were U.S. Champions for three years straight in what's called International Modern 5-Dance. It's one of the toughest competitions, and includes the slow waltz, foxtrot, quick step, tango, and the Viennese waltz. Andy and I started going with them to the comps when we were babies. I grew up with music in my veins and the soft brush of dancers' feet across a wood floor vibrating through my bones. I learned to walk on a waxed ballroom floor.

I caught Joe smirking at me as Dad and I took dance

position. I gave Joe a look back that said, *Watch this, wise guy! You'll change your tune.*

The music was already playing—good old Tony belting out "Let's Face the Music and Dance."

Appropriate, I thought wryly.

A second later, all I could think of was following Dad through the complex pattern of heel turns, weaves, spins and sweeping movements across the floor. Surrounding us was a blur of wide eyes and surprised smiles. No one was making funny faces any more. Not even Joe.

When the music stopped, Dad whirled me away from him and into a low curtsy while he bowed. The students clapped wildly. Half of them would sign up for the next level of lessons as soon as they could hurry to my mother's desk, which was exactly what my father had planned.

I walked off the floor without looking back. I'd made my point, there was nothing more I needed to say to Mr. I-Can-Do-Anything.

Before I'd gone five steps, a hand caught my arm and spun me around. "Hey, why didn't you tell me that's what we're supposed to look like!" Joe said, laughing.

I shook my head at him. "You were having a tough time not stepping on your own feet, and you want me to talk advanced technique with you?"

"Come here, party pooper," he said, and dragged me into his arms.

"Stop it." I tried to push him away. He was strong. Very strong.

My father had put on music so students could stay after class and practice. That was apparently what Joe intended to do, with or without my cooperation.

"It's more like this, isn't it?" he asked.

69

He bent his knees, squared his shoulders, and raised his chin in the air then took off across the room in a fair imitation of a competitive foxtrot step. So what if he wasn't quite in time with the music. I caught a glimpse of us in the mirrors, and we actually looked pretty good.

I started laughing.

"What's wrong?" He stopped and glared at me. "I thought I was doing pretty okay."

"You were," I said, unable to stop giggling. "That's just it. I think your ego controls your feet more than your brain does."

His eyes darkened. "What's that supposed to mean?"

"Nothing." I turned away. Other students were watching us, and my mother was giving me an evil eye from her desk. The one that said, *Don't argue with, antagonize, or make fun of the students!*

"No, wait. I want to know what you meant by that crack."

I turned around and faced Joe. "I'm sorry, I didn't mean anything."

"Yes, you did," he insisted. "You meant I can't dance like you and your father because I've got a swelled head. Just because I said it was easy and anyone could do it, you're ticked off. That's it, isn't it?"

"Forget it," I whispered. "I'm sorry I said anything."

"No way!" His eyes flashed with determination. He looked as if he were standing on the free throw line, trying for a crucial two-pointer. "I'm going to make you admit you're wrong. If I wanted to do what your dad just did with you, I could. All I'd need is a little practice."

I stuck out my tongue at him.

I know it was a dumb kid's move, but who can argue rationally with a bragging jock, and win?

Joe cracked up, laughing. "I'll show you," he said, pointing a challenging finger at me. "I will!"

Red and Toup showed up at the studio about fifteen minutes later. They explained that they wanted to speak to me alone. My mother ushered us into the office then left with a worried expression in her eyes.

"What is this about your finding your missing things?" Red demanded, as soon as my mother closed the door behind her.

"I thought you'd want to know," I said in as normal a voice as possible. "The gown and CDs turned up in my locker last night."

The two cops just looked at me. Red made an impatient sound, down low in her throat. If she'd been a dog, it would have been a growl . . . and she'd have been a German shepherd, a *big, angry* German shepherd.

"Look, I know this sounds goofy, but I went back to school last night for a notebook I'd left there. When I opened my locker, the gown and CDs fell out. I have no idea how they got there."

"What about the money?" Toup asked. "The cash box?" I noticed for the first time what bushy eyebrows he had. He scrunched them up like little caterpillars over his eyes when he was concentrating hard, like now.

"No money," I said.

Red let out a long, doggy breath. "I don't suppose you want to tell us how the dress got from here to there."

"I told you, I don't *know* how it got in my locker!"

71

I groaned. "I knew you'd figure I'd made it all up, but I had to tell you, didn't I?"

Neither of them answered.

"Have you found any fingerprints in the antique shop?" I asked.

"Why?" Red asked.

"I thought maybe you could dust my locker, match the prints there with ones you found in Vivaldi's. Maybe narrow the field of suspects or something?"

"There were no fingerprints," Toup blurted out.

Red winced, as if she wasn't pleased he'd let slip this juicy bit of information. "Most everything in the shop had been wiped clean of prints," she explained reluctantly. "The only ones we found were on a few display cases, and they belonged to Mrs. Hemingway or Miranda."

"Oh," I said.

"Where are the items?" she asked. "Your dress and CDs . . ."

"In the next room. I'll get them for you."

When I came back into the office the two cops were talking quietly but cut short their conversation and turned toward me with blank expressions. They probably couldn't figure out what to make of me, turning in reports of stolen goods, showing up with them days later.

"Are you sure there isn't anything you want to tell us about the night Miranda died?" Red asked.

"I didn't kill her. I couldn't kill anyone," I said as forcefully as possible.

She didn't look convinced. "Do you have a lot of friends?" she asked as she examined the peach-colored dress.

"No more than anyone else," I said cautiously. Where was she headed now?

Red glanced at her notepad, lying on my father's desk. "Diana Stewart and Tammy Mann are very close to you. Right?" She looked me straight in the eye this time.

"Yes, we're best friends, the three of us."

"And would you do anything for them, anything that would help them do well in school, say, or in their hobbies?"

"Of course."

"Would they do the same for you?" Toup asked.

I narrowed my eyes at him. Apparently, this was a line of questioning they'd discussed while I was out of the room. "They wouldn't do anything illegal, if that's what you're getting at. They wouldn't knock off one of my opponents so I could win the Mid-Atlantics."

"They might not have *wanted* to kill her," he pointed out. "They might have planned to just tap her hard enough to leave her with a good-sized headache."

"Or a mild concussion," Red added hopefully.

I thought about my friends. Diana had a warped sense of humor sometimes, and she didn't like Miranda any more than I did. But she was basically a pacifist. I'd seen her rescue a cat from a couple of boys who were tormenting it. For her effort, the cat had viciously scratched her face when she lifted it out of the garbage can in which they'd been rolling it around. All she'd said as she wiped away the blood was, "Poor thing, it must have been scared to death."

Tammy was either flying high and talking about how the world was full of wonderful possibilities, or she was ready to give up and become a street person. She alternately went on food binges and starvation diets. You could never predict her moods.

But she usually was harder on herself than on other people. Although I remembered the time we'd seen Miranda trip a freshman who couldn't swim, making her fall into the deep end of the pool. Tammy stole Miranda's clothes and locked her in the girls' showers. The janitor had found her three hours later.

"No," I said at last. "Neither of them would have done anything to hurt Miranda, even if they thought it would help me."

Red nodded.

Toup scribbled in his notebook. I wondered why they both took notes. Maybe they compared them later.

"The boy you met outside the studio that night, Joseph Ernst, the one who's *not* your boyfriend," Red said. "Did you see which way he was coming from?"

"Which way?"

"Yes, was he coming from the east end of the street or the west, or across the street from the direction of the antique store?"

I shook my head, confused. "I don't remember. He was just there all of a sudden. But that doesn't matter," I added quickly. "Remember, he was standing *with* me when the killer drove off in Miranda's car."

"We don't know her killer was driving that car. And we don't know that there was only one person involved," Red said.

Were they saying that Joe might have done it, and a partner drove off in the car, giving him an alibi? I thought about the great-looking basketball player—how honest he was about everything. He just came right out and said things that most people wouldn't dream of saying.

"Getting involved in something like this doesn't sound like him at all," I said at last.

"But you told us before that you don't know him very well," Red pointed out, drilling me with a sharp look.

I shrugged. There didn't seem to be anything I could say that they wouldn't pick apart. I was getting worried. I kept eliminating suspects for them, and all they had left was *me*!

I didn't want to go to prison for something I didn't do. In prison, no one dances.

"We'll take the dress and CDs," Toup said, suddenly taking charge. "That's all for now."

"Can I have my dress back soon?" I asked. "It's for a competition, and—"

Then I remembered I still didn't have a partner.

"Never mind," I said. It was hopeless. Who was I kidding? "I guess you can keep it as long as you need it."

9 *That night, I stayed late* again at the studio, even though I didn't have homework. I needed to be alone to think.

Was it possible, one of the theories that Red and Toup were suggesting—that someone *I knew* had killed Miranda, thinking he or she was helping me?

As I locked the door behind my parents, promising I'd get a ride home from Andy, I thought about Diana, Tammy, and now, Andy himself.

When we were competing, he'd stop off at the studio after work, and we'd go over a few steps before going home. That made for late school nights, but we both seemed to do okay on five or six hours' sleep, and my parents didn't care as long as we kept up our grades. To them dancing was a profession, and as important as school.

Andy, I mused, had seemed initially shocked by Miranda's death but wasn't acting overwhelmed by grief. And I'd thought he might be in love with her . . .

I pulled a chair up to one of the windows facing Allegheny and looked across the street at the antique store. All the lights were off. I knew the place was locked up tight. Miranda's aunt, Cassandra Hemingway, hadn't opened for business since the murder.

My thoughts shifted away from Andy, and I wondered how Mrs. Hemingway was taking her niece's death. And how about Miranda's parents?

What a horrible thing, for someone in your family to die. I pictured my parents, standing side by side and cheering as they watched me dance in every comp I'd entered since I was little. What would I ever do if something happened to one of them, or to Andy? My stomach suddenly felt queasy, and I forced the dark images out of my mind.

Gradually, I became aware of a faint glow from behind one of the windows across the street. I frowned, at first convinced I was seeing nothing more than the reflection of a street light in the glass. But the light shifted and seemed to grow brighter, then faded again.

It looked as if someone was walking around inside the shop with a flashlight.

Jumping up, I ran for my suede jacket on the coat stand beside my mother's desk and swung the door closed behind me. The new keys were in my purse, which was slung over my shoulder. I could get back in tonight if I needed to.

I wasn't sure what I hoped, or feared, I'd find in Vivaldi's, or what I'd do when and if I did find it. But if someone was in there, I could find a way in too. I thought I should call the police, then decided not to. I wanted to look around inside for myself first. Anyway, they probably wouldn't believe me.

I flew down the three flights of stairs, the suede fringes on my jacket dancing wildly from my arms, and out the front door onto the sidewalk. A few cars passed by in the street. A man and woman stood on the nearest corner, arguing about something that had happened in a restaurant. I could catch only a couple of their words: ". . . lousy service . . . soup . . . no one knows . . ."

I crossed the street and, looking to make sure no one was watching me, tried the front door of the shop. It was locked.

The alley, I thought unenthusiastically. I envisioned mice, or worse, rats scurrying across my path in the dark . . . or worst of all, whatever had been there before and chased me away. With a shiver, I slipped around the corner into the deeper shadows.

My eyes adjusted too slowly to the dark. I stepped on an empty soda bottle, twisting my ankle as it skittered crazily away from me then clinked hollowly against a trash bin. Catching myself against the brick wall, I hobbled on, feeling more like a professional klutz than a championship dancer.

"If music was playing, I'd be a regular James Bond," I muttered to myself.

There were no windows on the alley side of the building, so I couldn't keep track of the light. I knew of only two ways into the antique shop, the front door and the alley entrance. It was unlikely that anyone with evil intent would walk in or out of the street doors, in plain sight. So I figured I had the only other exit covered.

I followed the line of the wall farther back from the street. No car was parked here tonight. A single light bulb was screwed into a socket above the door, but it wasn't lit.

Holding onto the iron railing, I slowly climbed the cement steps. Dank air filled my lungs and I held it inside me, quieting my heart and listening. If that door above me swung open suddenly, it would knock me straight back down the stairs and I'd break my neck.

The door didn't open.

I reached for the knob and turned it. The cold metal sphere moved easily in my hand, and I felt suddenly unsure of myself.

If the door had been locked, I'd have had no choice but to leave. Now I had to go inside. I had to see who was there, because it might be the person who'd killed Miranda. He might have come back to look for something he'd left behind, something incriminating.

I swung the door open, just inches, and slipped through the crack, letting the heavy metal close quietly behind me.

More than anything, I wanted to turn around and rush back outside. But I reminded myself that I had a very good reason for being there. It wasn't fair that someone had killed Miranda. Even if she'd been the worst person on earth, she wouldn't have deserved to die. And, on a more personal note, if I didn't find out who *had* killed her, I might end up staring at the inside of a jail cell for a very long time, which would make missing the Mid-Atlantics feel like a vacation!

Every time I talked to the two cops investigating Miranda's murder, I could see it in their eyes. They didn't seem to have any evidence against me yet, but if they found even one of my fingerprints in the wrong place, they'd come after me, thrilled they'd found someone to blame for the murder. A lot of the neighborhood merchants were very upset. There was talk about a crime wave in Towson. Things wouldn't calm down until Miranda's killer was found.

The thin glow of a light from the next room drew my eye and attention. Someone *was* in there, and they didn't want to be seen.

79

I remembered my mother's words: *Desperate people do desperate things.*

Careful. Careful, I thought.

As I moved across the crowded storage room, I pretended I was threading my way through a crowd of dancers during a competition. Paintings in paper wrappers, wooden crates, and dusty furniture were stacked everywhere. The room smelled of lemon oil and the mustiness that all old things hold inside of them. My fingers brushed something cobwebby. I opened my mouth but swallowed the scream when I saw that it was only the filmy tulle of an old petticoat.

The light in the other room had come to a stop now. I froze, hoping the person holding it hadn't heard me. Maybe he was listening for my footsteps, maybe his heart was pounding as raggedly as mine was. It seemed almost comical—two people sneaking around in the dark, trying to avoid each other but wanting to know who the other one was.

I took another step. The light suddenly went out.

I swallowed. *Now I've had it*, I thought. *He knows I'm here.*

There was absolute silence, the only light from the street lamps outside the front windows. Hoping I'd be less visible if the intruder looked into the storage room, I dropped to my hands and knees. There was a soft scuffling noise, then the sound of a latch clicking into place.

Then silence again.

Whoever had been there must have left.

I breathed out and squeezed my eyes shut for a moment, trying to think what I should do. Leaving would be the safest choice. But leaving wouldn't give me evidence to convince the police I hadn't lied about the burglary at the studio, hadn't knocked off Miranda.

Moving back into the main part of the shop, I looked around. There were lamps all around, some of them plugged in, and long, fluorescent overhead tubes—but I didn't want to light up all of Allegheny Street. Then I saw Mrs. Hemingway's desk in the back corner. On it sat a small brass lamp with a green glass shade. I turned it on.

The little lamp cast a comforting glow over the roomful of old furniture and the glass cabinets displaying antique jewelry and knickknacks. A rack of vintage clothing ran along one wall. A refinished oak bed and matching dresser with ornate pulls and a fresh coat of wax gleamed from the middle of the room.

A carved wooden figurehead of a woman, with flowing hair that almost covered her naked breasts, jutted into the middle of the room. She looked like something off the prow of an old sailing ship, and I wondered who in their right mind would buy something like that.

Near me stood a velvet-covered chaise. On its wine-colored cushions was a sign that said, Don't Sit on Me!

"Don't worry, I won't," I whispered.

The shop was more than a little strange because most of the stuff was truly ugly or of questionable taste. I remembered my mother telling my father, one day, that Cass Hemingway knew less about antiques than she did about dancing, and the woman didn't know a waltz from a cha-cha. She'd inherited the shop a few years earlier from her father, and since that time, my mother claimed, had made a remarkable mess of it.

But here and there, something wonderful—a rich painting, a crystal vase, a glittering bracelet that might have had real stones in it—caught my eye. Maybe

Mrs. Hemingway had stumbled on a few treasures.

Miranda had worked there before her aunt had taken it over. She might have known more about the business than Cassandra. Thinking of Miranda, I looked around with a chill. I didn't know what I'd expected to find—the chalk outline of a body, a blood stain scarring the floor—but there was no sign that a girl had been murdered in this place only a few days ago.

I stayed inside the reassuring circle of light from the desk lamp, touching items lightly as I passed them, working my way slowly across the room toward a second back room. This one had more open space in it and seemed to be kept in better order. There was a large table, clear of the junk that crammed the other room. At one end was another of the ship's figure-heads, this one even larger, maybe seven feet tall. The heavy wooden mermaid was riddled with worm holes, and just as buxom as her sister in the other room. I grinned. Three-foot boobs. Crazy sailors.

There was a door, so I stepped inside and closed it. The latch made a similar click to the one I'd heard a few minutes earlier. I turned on the overhead light, now that I was sure it couldn't be seen from the street.

File cabinets ranged along one side of the room, opposite the mermaid. The table was rough, and looked as if it had been recently used as a workbench, maybe for restoring some of the antiques in the shop.

My foot hit something, and the object flew across the floor, rattling to a stop against the base of the file cabinets. I crossed the room and stooped to pick it up. A lightweight paintbrush.

Why would they use a paintbrush like this in Vivaldi's? I wondered. It wasn't the wide, flat type used to apply varnish to furniture. It was a fine-tipped artist's brush. I stood up slowly, studying it.

The sound behind me was so soft I almost didn't hear it at all. It took my brain a moment to register that it was a footstep, something I should definitely worry about. I turned slowly as a low, groaning creak grew louder. When I looked up, the worm-pocked chest of the mermaid was falling toward me, fast.

"No!" I screamed, leaping to one side.

But it was too late. The massive wooden figure crashed down on my shoulder, pinning me momentarily to the table. Then both the mermaid and I glanced off the rough corner. With a thunderous boom, everything seemed to collapse around me.

10

I was there, but I wasn't *really* there.

That's the only way I can describe the feeling of being unconscious, or semiconscious, or whatever I was when the voices started creeping into my head. The world was a murky gray-green, swirling with darker shadows of the deepest black. An enormous weight felt as if were lifting from my chest, then someone moved my body and a sharp pain shot through my shoulder.

My brain shouted, "Scream!"

But no words escaped from my lips.

My eyes refused to open, even when I wanted desperately to see what was going on around me . . . who was moving me.

It's him! The one who pushed over the mermaid! I thought wildly, and a ripple of terror tore through every nerve in my body.

I couldn't let him finish me off! Unfortunately, I wasn't exactly in prime physical condition for flight.

Rough hands lifted me again, and I tightened up in fear.

"Stop! Don't touch me! It hurts!" Mr. Brain yelled.

Still, no sound came out.

"It's all right, Carrie. We've got you," a familiar voice said. It was a deep, soothing voice—a guy's. I liked it.

We who?

I concentrated hard on my lips. A feeble grunt came out.

"Call an ambulance," the soothing voice ordered.

"I don't know the number."

"9-1-1, you jerk!"

"Oh yeah."

Something soft came up under me as supporting hands slipped out from beneath my shoulders.

"Ow!" I shrieked.

"Sounds like she's coming out of it," the familiar voice said.

"Brilliant deduction, Joe, old man."

My eyes flashed open, and I decided I'd definitely died and gone to heaven. Six faces looked down at me. Each one was attached to a hunky body.

Joe Ernst leaned closer, pushing the other boys back. "What happened, Carrie?" he whispered.

I grinned at him dizzily, feeling a lot better. "Brought the whole team for a lesson?"

His face turned crimson.

"Lesson?" the boy behind him asked. I recognized Matt Donovan, the varsity basketball team's captain.

"She's delirious," Joe muttered.

"Oh ho," I teased, "you didn't tell them. Did you, twinkletoes?"

"Shut up!" he said, "or I'll roll you off this couch onto the floor."

I winced at the thought of more pain. My head was starting to clear, though. He'd asked what had happened. Good question, I thought.

"How did you guys get here?" I asked weakly.

85

"We were walking down the street from Strapazzi's, toward the parking lot, when we heard this humongous crash and a scream," Micky Johnson said.

"We didn't know it was you," Joe added.

"How did—" my voice caught on a fresh wave of pain as I tried to adjust my position on the couch.

"We took the direct route," Joe explained. "Through the display window."

"Oh great," I mumbled, picturing shattered glass all over Vivaldi's front showroom and the sidewalk outside. The police would be thrilled. So would Mrs. Hemingway.

"What were you doing in here?" Joe asked.

"I saw a light inside the gallery, and I came to investigate. I thought whoever was in here had run off, but I must have been wrong. I guess they didn't like me spying on them. They pushed the mermaid over on me."

"Geez," Joe breathed.

"It must have weighed a ton."

"Pretty close. It took four of us to lift it off of you." He studied me solemnly. "Why didn't you just call the police from the studio?"

I thought better of shrugging. "They're not in the mood to believe anything I say. Either they wouldn't have come at all, or they'd have figured I'd invented something again, and they'd show up already believing what they wanted to believe."

From a distance, I could hear the wail of an ambulance, growing louder. Then there was another siren. I groaned, laying my head back against the couch. Soon I'd be answering a lot more questions.

"And you're sure you didn't bump up against the figurehead and knock it over on yourself?" Red asked.

"No," I repeated tiredly. "I told you back at the emergency room, someone was in Vivaldi's when I got there. I thought I'd scared them off, but they must have closed one of the inside doors to make it sound like they were leaving."

Luckily they hadn't made me stay at the hospital. I was home in my own bed, in my own room, and being there had never felt so good. I snuggled down beneath the covers.

"Carrie, why do you think anyone would try to hurt you?" Toup asked.

I rolled my eyes. It seemed pretty obvious to me. "Because I'm nosing around, because I found a clue that might lead you to Miranda's killer."

"What clue is that?"

I hesitated. I'd been thinking about the paintbrush, but now I wasn't sure that it meant anything at all. Maybe I'd seen something else in the gallery, something very important that my attacker didn't want me to be able to tell anyone about. The problem was, I didn't know what that something was.

I sighed and looked up at my mother. She and my father had stayed with me the whole time I was at the hospital, while the doctor examined me, while the technicians took X rays, and the doctor worked on my shoulder. The police had been there, too, asking their questions.

"I'm really tired," I murmured to my mother. "My shoulder's throbbing."

Mom nodded at me, as if to say, *That's all right. I'll take it from here.*

The doctor in the emergency room had taped my shoulder. I had dislocated it, he told me. It would hurt for a couple of weeks. He'd given me some pills to take when the pain got bad. My mother had made me take one, and it did help, but it also made me feel as if someone were spinning me around on a barstool.

The figurehead had also left some pretty gross looking bruises on my back and ribs. Otherwise I was okay.

"Carrie has told you everything she can for now," my mother informed Red and Toup. "Maybe tomorrow, after she's had some rest, she'll remember more of what happened."

Red glanced disappointedly toward the door, then back at me, as if she hungered to grill me for a few more hours. I must be holding something back. She'd make me crack.

My father gave the cops a stern look, and escorted them out of my bedroom.

As soon as they'd gone, my mother started fussing around the bed, tucking me in as if I was still two years old, moving the Kleenex box and glass of water closer to me, fluffing my pillow. She looked pale and her eyes were dull. Her hands trembled slightly as she brushed the linens smooth.

"I'm okay, Mom," I whispered sleepily. "Really."

"Yes," she said, touching me lightly on the forehead. "It was just so . . . so frightening."

"I know. For me too."

I felt her floating above me, her silence full of her own questions.

"I'm not making up any of this stuff. You have to believe me." I closed my eyes. "I didn't do anything to hurt Miranda, and I didn't fake a ton of driftwood falling on top of me."

"Oh, I know, dear. I was just thinking that competition is very stressful," she said softly. "Maybe your father and I have pushed you and Andrew too hard."

"You didn't push at all. I love to dance! If you told me I couldn't, I'd do it anyway."

She sighed and bent down to brush her lips across my cheek. "I suppose you would, stubborn little girl that you are."

"I'm not a little girl," I protested weakly, and drifted off into a candy-pink, pill-induced haze.

When I woke up, sunlight was streaming through my window. Like every morning, the first thing I thought of was dancing. But, today, the second thing I thought of was my injured shoulder, which was throbbing annoyingly. It struck me that I wouldn't be doing much dancing with my arm taped to my body.

Gingerly, I experimented with moving the shoulder joint. Pain radiated through the bones in every direction.

I bit down on my lip and waited for the fire to go away. Then I remembered the doctor saying something about hot showers, and gentle stretching exercises after a few days. I looked over at the bedside table and saw the page of instructions he'd left for me—stick figures marched across it, demonstrating funny positions.

I took a shower and felt a lot better. But I sensed the improvement wouldn't last. Maybe if I took a shower every couple of hours?

By the time I got dressed and had something to eat, it was 2:00 P.M. School would be getting out soon. There was no sense trying to go. I could call Diana after she got home to find out assignments for the classes we shared.

The house was empty. Mom and Dad had evidently left for the studio. Andy would be heading for the school parking lot soon, leaving for the mall. I enjoyed having the house to myself, moving around slowly, like someone visiting a stranger's home. I suddenly felt lucky, as if I were leading a charmed life. I'd survived what could have been a killing blow from a mermaid!

I giggled, but sobered up soon enough. The figurehead might have easily crushed me to death if it had fallen straight on top of me. I remembered the sturdy work table and heavy steel file cabinets I'd been standing in front of. They must have deflected the blow. Even so, it had apparently taken four guys to lift the mermaid enough for Joe to pull me to safety.

Deciding that nothing could happen to make this a bad day, I dressed in jeans and a loose purple sweater. It took me a long time to pull up my jeans with one hand and wiggle into my sweater. My shoulder didn't hurt as long as I didn't try to move it. I tucked the sweater's empty sleeve down inside. It made me look as if I had only one arm. I ate a late breakfast of an English muffin with strawberry jam slathered thickly over it, and drank down a tall glass of icy milk. Draping my suede jacket over my taped shoulder, I stuck my good arm through the sleeve and walked outside, into a beautifully cloudy fall day.

I wouldn't have cared if it started pouring.

On my way to the studio, I made a second decision. No matter what the police thought, the person who'd killed Miranda must be getting very nervous. He was so worried I'd find out his identity, he was willing to kill a second time.

As I walked I tried to think about all the people Miranda had snubbed, cheated on, or hurt in any way. The list was long, but when I really stopped to think about who she might have offended so badly they'd

want to kill her, I couldn't come up with one name.
Not *one* name!

On the other hand, if I were forced to choose someone who'd gain by her death, *my* name was at the top of the list of suspects.

I could see why Red and Toup were focusing their investigation on me.

"Hey, didn't think I'd see you up and around today!" a voice shouted from across the street.

I looked up, startled out of my grim thoughts. Joe and Matt were on the opposite side of Allegheny Street.

Matt whispered something to Joe. They laughed and started across the street toward me.

"What was that all about?" I asked.

"Nothing," Joe murmured, smiling at me. "You're really okay? The doctor says you can be up and around?"

"He said I should get some rest, and no one was home to stop me from getting up."

Joe frowned. "That's not quite the same as getting the doctor's permission to go out."

"I feel fine," I assured him. All I needed was a little shoulder transplant. "Are you coming for the lesson tomorrow night?"

His mouth tightened and eyes darted meaningfully toward Matt. "Uh, lesson?"

I felt like giving him a hard time. "Duh, your *dance* lesson. You know, the Wedding Survival class?"

Matt grinned wickedly. "You gotta be kidding! Him, dance?" He elbowed Joe in the ribs. "You think the star forward of Mencken High's varsity team would be seen in some prissy dance studio?"

Joe let out a derisive laugh. "Yeah—fat chance."

I glared at him, suddenly furious. He'd sworn to me

he didn't care what people thought. He'd made me like him—but he was still trashing the most important thing in my life.

"You jerk!" I spun around and marched down the sidewalk, turning into the lobby of the Dying to Dance building.

Guys! I thought. Why did they all have such massive macho hang ups?

I pushed the elevator button and waited . . . waited . . . waited, cradling my left arm to support my throbbing shoulder. I'll take the stairs, I decided, and turned to retrace my steps down the hallway. I ran into Joe coming from the other direction.

"Get out of my way!" I growled.

"I'm sorry," he said. "I really am."

"Sorry about what? Slamming my dream?"

He winced, then jumped aside when I didn't stop and would have plowed right through him. "Listen, Carrie, I had to say something to get Matt off my back. Besides, guys just don't waltz and foxtrot and do stuff like that these days. It looks weird to most people, you know?"

"No, I don't know." I swung open the stairway door and rushed through it onto the steps.

"Carrie!" he shouted after me.

I heard him running up the steps behind me, but I didn't stop. I'd had to make excuses for my dancing all of my life. I wasn't going to do it any more.

"Carrie!" He was gaining on me, taking two steps to my one.

"Go away!" I yelled. My shoulder was hurting badly, but I didn't want to stop or listen to his lame explanations.

I felt his hand seize the fringes of my jacket, and I

wheeled around to faced him, madder than a wet cat. "Let go, you'll ruin my jacket!"

"No, listen to me."

"Get lost!" I shouted. "And don't bother showing up for any more lessons."

"You don't understand—"

"I *do* understand!" I was breathing hard, trying to restrain myself from smashing him in the face with my fists. Maybe I was overreacting, but I couldn't help it. His sort of attitude had hurt me too many times before. I clenched and unclenched my fists until my knuckles ached. "You're afraid your friends on the team will think you're a wimp because you take dance lessons."

"Carrie, I said I was s—"

I didn't let him finish. "Well, if they tried my kind of dancing, they'd know wimps can't handle it. Swing dancing for fifteen minutes straight is like sprinting two miles. Andy and I both lift weights to build stamina and muscle tone."

Joe looked blankly at me.

What difference does it make? I thought, throwing up my good hand. The whole day and my wonderful mood were totally ruined.

"Just leave me alone," I said tiredly. "If you're afraid of what your friends think, maybe you should start checking with them before you make any important decisions."

"That's not fair," he said tightly.

"Tell me about it."

Joe grabbed my hand before I could climb any further. Pulling me down to sit on a step, he lowered himself beside me.

"I'm sorry," he murmured. "You're right, I shouldn't listen to them. But you know, the whole team will be on me once Matt starts spreading the word.''

I took a deep breath, calming down a little. I understood how he felt. "Do you like dancing?'' I asked.

"Yeah,'' he said slowly, sounding surprised at his answer.

"Then forget about them.''

For all the fuss these days about liberating the sexes and alternative roles, guys still didn't want to admit they liked anything graceful or romantic.

I grinned at Joe, but nicely this time. "You're a big boy. I guess you can make your own decisions.''

He gave me an odd look. "You know what I'd really like to do?'' he asked.

"What?''

"I'd like to take some private lessons in between the group classes.''

I laughed at him, shaking my head. "You don't have to try to impress me. Just finish the last two classes your mother paid for, to make her happy. Then the pain is over.''

"I'm serious,'' he said. "I started out giving you a hard time because it was easy to do. That was one way to get you talking to me. I guess I got carried away.''

"You could have said, 'Hi, it's a nice day.' I'd have talked to you then, too.''

"I liked getting you mad,'' he confessed, his voice sounding a little husky. His blue eyes rose to meet mine.

I frowned at him. "Why?''

"Because you're pretty when you get emotional about something.''

I felt my cheeks growing hot and, probably, bright

pink. I was glad the stairwell was kind of dark. *Be reasonable*, I told myself.

"Be reasonable," I said out loud.

"Huh?"

"I mean, taking private lessons doesn't make any sense for you. It's expensive, and what will you do after you learn to dance like Astaire? Dee jays don't play waltzes and tangos at the school dances."

"Towson State has a swing night once a month. It's open to the public and might be fun . . . you know, if I had someone to go with who was a good dancer." He looked straight into me, and I felt my bones melt.

"Oh," I forced out.

"So, what do you say? Will you teach me?"

"*Me?*" I gasped.

"Yeah, why not?"

I pushed up off of the stairs. "I don't usually teach private lessons."

Actually, my parents thought I was still too young, even though I was dying to start. Most students were in their thirties or older, and my folks believed adults didn't like being taught by a high school student. But I was a better dancer than most of the part-time instructors they hired.

"I'll think about it," I said and started up the stairs again. "You know, maybe we can work out a deal about the cost."

"How much is it?"

"Normally, forty-five dollars an hour."

Joe whistled. "That's steep."

I forgot I couldn't and lifted my shoulders. Clamping a hand over my upper arm, I waited for the pain to go away. "I was thinking," I gasped, "I have to keep in shape and work on a few steps for the Mid-Atlantics. With any luck I'll find a new partner in a week or so, and my shoulder will heal fast. In the meantime, I have to keep practicing. That's hard to do without someone to work out with."

Joe grinned as if he liked the idea. "You mean me? That'd be fun!"

"No, it won't," I told him with ghoulish pleasure. "What I'm going to do to you, you won't like at all!"

It was after midnight, and I was still feeling pleased about Joe, when Mom knocked on my bedroom door and stepped into my room. I took one look at her face and sat up straight on the bed.

"What's wrong?"

"Have you seen Andy tonight?" she asked.

"No, wasn't he supposed to work after school?"

"Yes," she said vaguely. "But he hasn't come home yet."

While I was still at the studio, I'd finished the homework Diana had given me over the phone. After I'd gotten home, I spent the next hour planning steps I could teach Joe, actually working up a little routine he could learn fairly quickly.

I knew he was too impatient to stay with the simplest steps in the bronze syllabus, which was the list of beginner steps. So I put a bunch of them together with a few from the silver level, to make it more interesting for him. Although I'd heard my father say a million times there's no such thing as a born dancer, I knew that some students learned very slowly, while others seemed to catch on fast.

Maybe because Joe was so involved in sports, so in tune with his own body, he was able to pick up steps pretty fast. The night he'd mimicked my father by dancing with me after class, I'd been shocked at how close he'd come to getting the footwork down on the first try. I found myself looking forward to dancing with him again.

I smiled dreamily, then caught my mother's worried expression and pushed thoughts of Joe from my overheated brain.

"Maybe Andy dropped by a friend's house on the way home," I suggested. "It's only a little after twelve."

"I just got off the phone with the Johnsons and the Donovans. I woke up both families, calling at this hour. No one has seen Andy tonight."

I tossed off the covers and thrust my feet into my slippers then crossed the room quickly, heading for the phone downstairs. "I'll call some of the girls in his class," I offered.

An hour later, I'd had no luck calling around, and Andy still hadn't shown up. He'd told me that he sometimes he drove around at night, to clear his head, just for a half hour or so. He'd never stayed out this late, though. I began to get a tight feeling in my stomach.

Someone had tried to kill me last night, and now my brother was missing. I hoped the two incidents weren't related, but I had an awful feeling that they were.

None of us were able to sleep that night. My mother, father, and I sat around the table, drinking black coffee and listening to the clock over the stove click off the minutes.

I thought about Miranda's death, how it had happened while I was only steps away from her, and what had happened to me since then.

There seemed to be two obvious possibilities. Either her murder was planned to make me look guilty—so

97

that she and I and the murderer were tied together from the beginning, in some way I didn't yet understand. Or her death was what the newspapers called "a random act of violence." She just happened to be in the wrong place at the wrong time. Someone broke into Vivaldi's Collectibles, just like they'd broken into the studio, looking for cash or anything else of value.

The only trouble with Theory #2 was that anyone in their right mind had to realize there wouldn't be much worth stealing in a dance studio. Shoes? A bunch of checks written for lessons? Why break into a dance studio when on the same street there was a jewelry store, a furrier, three popular restaurants, and an antique store loaded with jewelry and pricey paintings? It just didn't make sense, especially when you considered the reappearance of my peach gown! Why steal something, then give it back?

So that left Theory #1, which meant that Miranda had been killed intentionally, for some reason no one had yet figured out. And it couldn't be a coincidence that, ever since her death, things had happened that kept leading the police to me. Someone was manipulating evidence. Someone was watching me and was making sure that the police remembered Miranda and I had been sworn enemies (at least on the dance floor).

Someone had stolen my gown while Miranda was still alive, then planted it in my locker after she was dead. What was that word lawyers used in murder trials? *Premeditated*. That meant someone had planned to kill the person, it wasn't just something that happened by accident.

Someone had tried to kill me in the antique store, or at least leave me pinned under the mammoth mermaid so that the police would know I'd been snooping around the scene of Miranda's murder.

I wondered if Red and Toup believed in the old saying, *The criminal always returns to the scene of the crime.*

And now Andy was missing.

I couldn't help feeling that his disappearance must somehow tie in with everything else.

I wrapped my good arm around my ribs. Suddenly I felt cold, very cold . . . and very afraid. I had been wrong. Today hadn't been a lucky day at all.

My father coughed into his hand and stood up from the kitchen table when the clock read 3:00 A.M. "I'm calling the police," he announced.

My mother started to cry.

11 *I pushed myself up and* away from the table as soon as my father hung up the phone.

"Where are you going?" my mother asked. Her eyes fixed on me worriedly as she blew her nose into a paper napkin. "The police will be here soon."

"Like they're going to produce my brother when they couldn't find a stolen dress or the person who clobbered me with a seven-foot mermaid!"

"Don't get smart-mouthed," my father warned tightly.

"Sorry," I said. He looked like he was about to crack under the tension, too.

"I'm going to call Joe," I told him. "Maybe another guy will have some ideas where to look for Andy."

My brother was pretty simple. His whole world revolved around four locations: school, the studio, the mall, and our house. You could always find him in one of those places, or somewhere in between.

It was very unusual for him to not turn up where he was supposed to be. Since the first three possibilities were closed for the night—that left *home*. By all the laws of the Clark Universe, he should have been here.

I looked up Joe's number in the high school telephone directory.

His phone rang and I prepared my apologies to his parents for calling so late. A little kid's voice answered, surprising me.

"The Ernst residence . . . hi! Who's this?"

I would have been amused if I hadn't been so worried about Andy. "This is Carrie Clark, is Joe there?"

"Joe Senior or Junior?"

"Junior, I guess."

"I'll go wake him up," said the cheerful voice that sounded about five years old.

There was a pause then some shouting in the background—Joe's father, I guessed. At last, a familiar voice came on the line. "Carrie? Is that you?"

"Yeah," I burst out breathlessly. "I'm sorry to wake up your family, but I need your help."

"Sure, what is it?"

"Andy never came home after work. My parents are sick with worry, and I'm afraid something terrible has happened to him."

"I'll be right over."

"It's 3:30 in the morning," I reminded him.

"I'll *be* there," he repeated.

I wasn't off the phone five minutes when I heard a car pull up out front. I thought it would be the police, but it was Joe. A Baltimore County patrol car pulled up right behind him.

I opened the front door and let everyone in.

"It took you a long time to get here," my father said to Toup as he followed Andy through the door.

"We have other work besides keeping track of your family, Mr. Clark," the sergeant muttered.

101

Red gave him a "cool it" look.

I decided to ignore them, and pulled Joe into the dining room.

"Where would you go if you were Andy and you wanted to be alone for a while?"

He frowned, thinking. "Does he have his car?"

As if my father had just asked the same question, I heard Red, in the other room, say, "We came past the mall on our way here. Checked the few cars left in the parking lot after closing. Your son's wasn't there."

"His car isn't here, so he must be driving it," I whispered to Joe. My throat was so tight and dry, I could hardly force out the words. "But he always comes straight home. I think something terrible has happened to him."

Tears blurred my vision. I didn't want to cry in front of anyone, especially Joe. Turning away, I stared out the window at the dark street.

Joe put a comforting arm around me. "He'll turn up."

"But what if he doesn't? Or what if he turns up, but he's—"

"Don't think like that," he said gently. "He might have driven out of town, north toward Bel Air or west toward Frederick, on the back roads. Late at night, no one's on the road, you can drive real fast. Cleans out the brain." It sounded as if he'd often done that himself.

"That's possible, I guess."

"Ask your mother if we can drive around for a while, check out a few places. There could be a simple explanation—like he had a flat or ran out of gas on a back road."

My spirits lifted just a little. Yes, that was a possibility. Andy might have been more upset about Miranda's death than I'd realized. He might have gone for a drive to sort out his feelings. That sounded like him.

If his car had broken down, there might be no phone, no gas station for miles. Andy might be hiking back toward the highway even now.

"I'll be right there," I said, almost smiling. "I'll just tell my parents we're leaving."

I ran into the living room where the two cops were sitting with my parents.

"Good, here she is," my mother said, as if they'd been talking about me.

Red looked at me, then back to my parents. "It would be better if we spoke to her alone."

My parents stood up, eager to please, as if their following official instructions guaranteed Andy's speedy return. I felt sorry for them and played along. If the police had a couple of quick questions, I'd get them out of the way, then Joe and I could leave.

"Sit down," Red said, as soon as my parents were out the door. *So much for quick discussions*, I thought.

I sat on the couch facing the two cops, who each occupied one of my mother's two matched wing chairs. They looked as if they had sprouted pale brocade angel wings from the shoulders of their blue uniforms.

"Tell us about your relationship with your brother," Red said.

I stared at her. "Isn't this wasting valuable time? Shouldn't you be out looking for Andy?"

"Please answer the question," Toup mumbled.

I sighed. "Andy's my brother. We're like any brother and sister," I responded woodenly.

Red shook her head. "That's not what your parents just told us, or your friends at school."

103

I felt as if I'd missed something very important. "I don't understand. What did they tell you about Andy and me?"

"Everyone we speak to says that you and Andy are very close, *unusually* close for a brother and sister. You've danced together in competitions since you were very young."

"So?"

"You trust each other?"

"Of course."

"And how would Andy feel if he thought you'd broken that trust?"

I shook my head, totally confused now. "What is this all about?"

"Answer Officer Landry's question," Toup said.

"If I did something mean to Andy, I think he'd be very surprised, then hurt and maybe angry."

They looked at each other.

Red continued in a calm voice. "So the same might be true if your brother broke your trust?"

"I guess . . ." Suddenly I knew what they were really getting at, and it horrified me. "Wait a minute! If you're trying to say I might have done something to hurt Andy—"

Red snapped her notebook closed. Toup's unemotional gaze shifted to the door, and I knew without looking that Joe had just come into the room.

He sat on the back edge of the couch behind me, and dropped a hand on my shoulder as if to say, *It's okay, don't let them rattle you.*

"We're not accusing you of anything," Red insisted. "But your brother is missing, and you and he have just had a serious falling out over your dancing career, which seems to be awfully important to you."

I glared at her. "I can't believe this!"

"It's true that he told you he was going to be dancing with Miranda Hemingway?" she asked.

"Yes, that's right, you already knew that. But I didn't kill Miranda because she'd snatched my partner, and I didn't do anything to my brother to punish him!"

Red leaned forward in her chair. Her eyes were green, as glittering and sharp as a cat's. She held a small object in her outstretched hand. "Is this yours?"

I looked down. It was my gold chain bracelet, broken between two links.

"Where did you find that?" I asked. I'd been wearing it the night before when I'd searched Vivaldi's. I hadn't even noticed that it was missing. It must have fallen off in the shop.

"It was in the mall parking lot," Toup said stiffly, "near the area where your brother usually parked, according to your parents."

My stomach knotted itself with a painful jerk. "I lost that bracelet before tonight, probably in Mrs. Hemingway's shop."

"You didn't report it missing," Red said.

I shouted, "I didn't know—"

Joe touched me on the shoulder. "She was almost crushed to death. You expect her to take inventory of her jewelry?"

Toup gave him a sly smile. "We're just curious why she suddenly claims to have lost a bracelet after it turns up in the parking lot where her brother was accosted."

"Accosted?" I repeated.

Red lowered her voice. "There were traces of blood on the pavement near the bracelet. The blood appears to be fresh."

I couldn't believe what I was hearing. I shot up out of my seat. "I'd never hurt Andy! *Never!*"

My parents appeared in the doorway. My father's face was gray. My mother looked as if she might fall over any minute.

"That's enough, officers," Dad snapped. "Carrie is the last person in the world to suspect of hurting anyone—especially her brother." He turned to me. "You don't need to answer any more questions until I call a lawyer."

"We haven't charged your daughter with anything," Red stated, standing up. "We're just interviewing her as we would any other family member."

My father is no dummy. He looked as if he were about to hit her. "You'd better leave now," he said through gritted teeth. "If you want Carrie, she'll be where you can find her. But the next time she speaks with you, it will be with a lawyer present."

I could have kissed Dad for putting them in their places. But a shadow of a doubt slipped into my mind. If my father believed I was completely innocent, would he have felt it necessary to protect me or call for legal help?

"I want to go look for Andy," I said as soon as the two cops left.

"No," my father said. "You stay here and let the police do their job. They'll find him."

"Will they?" I cried. "They haven't been doing so hot up to now." I was furious with them. They hadn't found Miranda's killer. Why should they be able to find Andy?

My father just shook his head.

"What about your brother?" Joe asked.

It was the next day, and we were standing in the middle of one of the little practice rooms flanking the ballroom at my parents' studio. Andy still hadn't shown up, and to take my mind off of his disappearance, Joe had called the house and asked for his first private lesson. I hadn't gone to school, and I didn't feel much like dancing. Joe had insisted.

"What about Andy?" I asked.

"Would your brother have any reason for taking your bracelet and making it look like he'd been the victim of foul play?"

"Don't be ridiculous. You're starting to sound like the police."

Joe reached out for me, but I stepped back and away angrily. I walked over to the window.

"Listen," he said in a voice I wasn't used to. It was gentle, with no hint of his usual teasing. "I know it's pretty tacky, talking about Andy as if he's some kind of nutcase, killing people, disappearing to make it look like something's happened to him."

"You're right," I spat out, "it's tacky and stupid."

"But *you* didn't kill Miranda," he said firmly.

Something about his confidence in me calmed me down a little. No one had come right out and said that—*You, Carrie Clark, didn't kill Miranda Hemingway.* Joe was stating a fact, something he believed in the way he believed in making free throws and playing a hard-fought basketball game.

I felt a gentle glow warm my insides.

"No, I didn't kill her," I said with a sigh. "But I know that Andy couldn't have, either."

"He had as much reason to want Miranda out of the way as you did," he pointed out. "Andy was half of your team. He could have pretended to want to dance with her, just to get close to her. He kills her, then you and he no longer have to compete with her.

"I know. I've thought about that. But even after

Miranda died, he stood by his decision not to come back and be my partner."

Joe thought for a moment. "That might have been to keep the police guessing. If he came right back to you, it might have looked bad."

"What about the gown and the bracelet? Both of those things were intentionally planted to make me look guilty. Andy wouldn't do something that terrible to me."

"I guess not," Joe murmured.

I stared out the window at Allegheny Street. It was late afternoon and still light. A lot of people were walking between shops and businesses and restaurants. I usually liked this time of day, after the energy of morning, before the evening classes began, when most of the students came. It was a time to take a break, relax before the day got busy again. My shoulder felt a little better. I went into the ladies' room and cut away the tape, then eased my arm into my shirtsleeve.

I heard Joe snap a cassette into the stereo. A racy Latin beat filled the small room. Almost without thinking, I walked back into the practice room, turned, and took dance position—my left hand on Joe's shoulder, my right hand in his left. I back-led him into a samba step, taking care not to jar my shoulder.

He followed my lead, catching on fast. We used more and more energy, making lots of crazy mistakes but ignoring them and keeping up with the lively beat.

If I danced hard enough and long enough, maybe it would take my mind off of Andy, off of the police and other people who didn't trust me. But at the end of the song, I was still too worried and scared to enjoy the adrenalin high of our dance.

"That was great!" Joe exclaimed, breathing hard.

"You didn't say a word, but you taught me a lot of cool steps just by doing them and letting me follow."

I turned away and leaned my forehead against the wall. "Something terrible has happened to Andy," I said, knowing absolutely that it was true. "I can't think about dancing or anything else until I find out where he is . . . how he is . . ."

"Let's go for that ride," Joe said.

I stared at him as if he were crazy. "My brother has been missing for almost twenty-four hours, and you think we're going to bump into him on a road somewhere?"

He shrugged. "It's better than doing nothing."

He was right.

We drove all around Towson, then west toward Reisterstown, then turned around and headed northeast into the countryside that eventually would lead into Pennsylvania.

"We can cover the main routes," I said disappointedly, after hours of driving and no sign of Andy or his car. "But we'll never drive past a tenth of the places he could have gone. This is hopeless."

Joe insisted on trying a little longer.

By the time we gave up, it was too dark to see much of anything.

That night on the late news, Baltimore's Channel 2 covered a crime story, and it took me a while to realize they were talking about Andy.

A young reporter stood outside the mall, speaking to the camera. "Police sources admit that carjacking is a possible motive behind the disappearance of a popular teenage boy from this parking lot last night. Andrew Clark, son of Milton and Genevieve Clark, owners of Dying to Dance Studio on Allegheny Street in Towson, has not been seen since ten o'clock last night.''

She stepped to one side and motioned toward the ground. "Andrew's 1990 Ford Escort is missing, and blood was found on the pavement near his usual parking spot.''

The camera zoomed in on a small section of cement. A dark stain filled the screen. I closed my eyes and swallowed three times, then twice more, sure I was going to throw up. *Andy's blood*, I thought. *Oh, God!*

The reporter babbled on. "Baltimore County police are asking anyone with information to call the police emergency hot line. The number is—''

I tuned out her voice. The screen showed a yearbook photo of Andy, his long hair pulled back so that you couldn't even tell it was long . . . the way he wore it for comps. I stared blindly at the TV screen.

"Oh, Andy!" I whispered, then the tears came and I couldn't stop crying.

The next morning our house felt like a funeral parlor. The shades had stayed drawn all the day before. The phone rang every fifteen or twenty minutes. My father answered each time in a low voice. I could hear him repeating his litany of, "No. No word yet. We'll let you know when we hear anything.''

Sometimes it wasn't a relative or neighbor, but someone from a newspaper or TV station. "We have no new news. How do you think it feels to not know if your son is alive?" Then he'd hang up on them.

It was disgusting. Who in their right mind asks someone who's lost a loved one how it feels? People can be so cruel.

It was Saturday. Normally, the studio wouldn't open until noon. I didn't know if Dad would go in to open up at all. I didn't know what to do with myself.

Red and Toup were leaving me alone, apparently frustrated because they couldn't find anything specific to incriminate me in either Miranda's death or Andy's suspicious disappearance. The lawyer Dad had hired telephoned and told us the police had completed the fingerprint and fiber tests they'd taken the day after Miranda's death. My prints weren't there, nor were there any fibers that matched up with clothes in my closet. I could imagine Red's eyes glowing a little dimmer when she got the news. She must have been disappointed.

Andy's disappearance seemed to be complicating the investigation. The cops acted as if Andy wasn't just missing, as if he was dead. But they must have admitted to themselves that it didn't make much sense for me to kill my own brother just for defecting to another dance partner.

None of that made me feel any better, however. Andy was gone, and my parents had started to talk about him in the past tense.

"Andy would have liked that movie on TV last night."

"Andy was always the first one to the phone."

"If Andy were here, we could at least play Monopoly to make the time pass . . ."

It's probably some kind of emotional safety valve. A way my parents were easing themselves into accepting a fact too horrible to imagine—that their son might be dead.

I hated it, and I couldn't stand listening to them for another minute. "I'm going to the studio," I said at the breakfast table. "I have some work to do."

"I'll meet you there around noon. We'll call before then, if we hear anything," my father promised. His voice sounded weak and his eyes were red-rimmed and watery, although he hadn't let me see him crying. I thought, *If there's a Hell, this is it.*

12 *I walked the scenic route* across town from our house to the studio. By cutting across two blocks, I came out opposite the courthouse and Baltimore County government offices. Their cool gray stone sparkled in the morning sunlight. The flower gardens between the two huge buildings were bright with gold, yellow, and red chrysanthemums.

I thought about what a pretty day it was, and how much Andy would have liked rollerblading across the park in the warm October sun. A wave of sadness washed over me, like the shadow of a storm cloud chasing away the sun.

I found myself on Tammy's street. She lived in a big old house that had been divided into four apartments. Her mom had liked the Victorian style of the place and once told me, "I could never afford to buy a house like this. Renting part of it is the next best thing."

I wondered how she managed to stay so upbeat about everything. Her husband had left her with three kids and moved out of state; no one knew where he was. So Mrs. Mann had to support the four of them on her own. But she was forever cheerful, finding something good in every day and every person.

"Sometimes my mother is so optimistic she makes me sick," Tammy had admitted. "Doesn't she *know* what a crummy thing he did to her . . . to all of us?"

There were days I wished Tammy had inherited more of her mom's lightheartedness. She could be as up as anyone one minute and lower than low the next. But even when she was down she went out of her way to help me if I needed her.

I was thinking about stopping at the Manns' place to cheer myself up when I spotted a girl a few houses down the street. She had long, permed hair, wore a tidy brown suit and sensible heels. Watching her as she loaded flat, rectangular packages into a car, I didn't at first recognize her.

"Isabelle, hi!" I called out as I got closer.

I remembered Tammy telling me that Isabelle's family lived just down the street from her.

Isabelle turned and squinted, as if trying to make out my face against the glare of the sun. "Hello," she said at last. She smiled shyly.

"You're up early," I commented. Few of my friends crawled out of bed much before noon on weekends, unless they had jobs.

"Yes." She glanced at the car. "I have to drive to Annapolis this morning."

I looked inside the backseat where she'd been stashing her packages. They stood in a neat row, on edge, so that the brown paper-wrapped rectangles looked like slices of bread wedged between the back of the driver's seat and rear bench.

"What are those?" I asked.

She shrugged. "Some paintings. I'm taking them to a gallery in Annapolis. They've offered to sell them for me."

114

"Really? That's great." I would have asked to see one, but they were so carefully wrapped I knew it would mean extra work for Isabelle to open it. "Are you going to sell any at the school craft show next month?"

Isabelle hesitated. "I don't think so. I can probably get more from a dealer."

"Wow, big time!" I said, smiling at her. It was nice to see someone so quiet and unassuming get credit for her hard work. Isabelle made me think of myself, back when I first danced in competitions. I'd been very timid about performing for judges. "What about your jewelry?"

"Maybe," Isabelle said, thoughtfully, "I haven't decided yet."

"I bought some earrings you designed, last year, for three of my cousins, and they adored them."

Isabelle's dark eyes gleamed with pride. "I'm glad they liked them. Maybe I will make more, if I have time." As she reached for another of the paintings propped against the car, a flash of gold on her finger caught my eye.

"Oh, you got your class ring!" I cried. "Let me see!"

Before Isabelle could pull her hand away, I grabbed it and held it up to study the ring. The stone was a brilliant crimson. Our school colors were red and gold, so garnet or topaz were the usual choices, but some students liked to use their birthstones instead. Isabelle had chosen the art club insignia for one side of the stone, while the madrigal choir symbol flanked the other side.

"It's beautiful," I said.

She smiled, looking pleased. "Thanks. I wanted one last year, but couldn't afford it." I remembered now that Isabelle was a senior. Most kids got their rings junior year. Mine was on order.

"It must be the eighteen-carat model," I commented, impressed. "It shines much brighter than . . ." I was about to say Andy's, but I couldn't bear to say his name. I swallowed over the lump in my throat. "It's just much brighter than some of my friends' rings."

"Oh no," Isabelle said quickly. "This is just the ten-carat ring, the cheapest one. The other was much too expensive for me."

"Oh," I said, hoping I hadn't hurt her feelings. I looked down the street. "I'd better get going." I hesitated. "Say, since you're going to be driving around today, would you do me a favor and keep an eye out for my brother's car."

"I heard about the thing at the mall on the radio," Isabelle said. "You must be awfully worried. I'm sorry." She looked sincerely upset.

"Thanks." I swallowed and blinked away the beginnings of tears. "The police say if we can locate his car, we may find a clue to where he is."

"I'll keep an eye out." She put the last picture into the car, then turned back. "I don't know what it looks like, his car I mean."

The TV reporter had mentioned the color and make, but I expected most people wouldn't remember. "He drives a '90 Escort. It's red, sort of faded, you know how they get."

"Right," she said.

"The license plate spells out his initials—ABC, Andrew Brian Clark. Call the police if you find it," I said.

"I will."

I was about to leave, thinking it had been really

dumb to ask her to look for Andy's car—what were the chances? Then another question came to mind.

"Miranda wasn't in art club, was she?" I asked, knowing that Isabelle had been vice president for three years.

She looked perplexed. "No, why?"

"Just wondering. I found a brush in her aunt's shop, and it didn't look like the kind someone would use for staining antique furniture."

"I don't think she was very good with art, or interested in it at all," Isabelle commented, then considered something for a moment. "Your friend Tammy is, though."

"Tammy?" I was surprised.

"Yes. She saw me sketching the other day and came over to watch. She mentioned trying her hand at oil painting some day."

I laughed. "Tammy gets a lot of wild ideas, but she doesn't often follow up on them."

Isabelle pursed her lips as if she was thinking about saying something, then closed them firmly.

"What?" I asked.

"Oh, it's none of my business."

"Of course it isn't, but tell me anyway," I teased, sounding more like Joe than myself. *I must be picking up some of his habits*, I thought.

She laughed self-consciously. "Well, I was just thinking how strange Tammy's been acting lately. Very . . . I don't know, off in a world of her own?"

"She's always like that."

"But she seemed awfully tense the last few days when I saw her leaving her house. I said hello to her and she didn't even answer. And she's getting really skinny, don't you think? She isn't bulimic or anything, is she?"

I hadn't even thought of giving her eating habits a name, but now that Isabelle had used the word, I wondered. Her food fetishes and mood swings fit what I'd read about some eating disorders. Sometimes she seemed super-charged emotionally, close to snapping. But I'd always figured it wasn't anything a good meal or staying off of brownies for a while couldn't fix.

Now I wondered. What was it Tammy had said that day about Miranda? About people thinking she deserved to die? Had *she* believed Miranda deserved to die?

"Maybe I should check on her," I said.

Isabelle nodded. "Good luck."

I turned to leave. Halfway down the sidewalk, I had the distinct feeling she was still watching me.

"I'm sorry," Isabelle called out before I reached Tammy's steps. "I'm really sorry about your brother."

I waved to her, unable to trust my voice not to crack.

118

13 *I knocked on Tammy's door,* but no one was at home. Maybe, I thought, there will be some time during the day when I can call her on the phone.

Isabelle had started me thinking about Tammy. She was right. I should have been more concerned about her. I'd been so busy preparing for the next comp, worrying about the police, then about Andy . . . I was ignoring a friend who might be in serious trouble. Then there was what she'd said about Miranda, about maybe her deserving what she'd gotten. That bothered me more and more the longer I thought about it.

Vivaldi's Collectibles normally opened at 10:00 A.M. on Saturdays, but I knew Mrs. Hemingway hadn't been in at all since Miranda's death. As I turned to enter our building, I glanced across the street and saw a man and woman looking through the display window that had just been replaced. They spoke to each other quietly, then pushed open the antique store's door and stepped inside.

I stopped and waited, but they didn't come right out. Apparently, Miranda's aunt was open for business. This, I decided, would give me a chance to look around in the daylight.

Unsure what I was going to do or say to Mrs. Hemingway, I crossed the street and let myself in through the front door. A tiny brass bell tinkled overhead.

Looking around, I spotted the couple standing at the glass counter near the back of the store, studying a case of antique brooches. Even from this distance, I could see that some of the pins were cameos, others held gemstones or colored crystals set in gold or silver. Mrs. Hemingway was so busy talking to the woman, she didn't notice me.

I strolled around the shop, looking at each section. When I'd been there the other night, everything had been in shadows and I couldn't make much of her stock. But today I could see that there seemed to be no organization at all to the items for sale.

Furniture, vases, paintings, and vintage clothing were displayed randomly, piled on top of each other. I didn't know much about antique periods and styles, but in other antique shops I'd visited with my mother, I'd noticed that one kind of furniture was usually grouped together. Often the smaller, more expensive pieces were set at the back of the store in glass cases, and fragile pieces of furniture were cordoned off so little kids wouldn't climb on them.

I remembered my mother's comments about Cassandra Hemingway's lack of knowledge of antiques, and waited while the couple haggled with her over the cost of a brooch. Miranda's aunt was maybe forty years old, about my parents' age. Unlike my mother, though, she was overweight and had a pasty complexion. Her hair seemed almost colorless and blended with her skin.

At last she appeared to tire of the discussion and said, "Oh well, if that's all you can afford, I'll settle for thirty dollars."

A surreptitious flash of victory passed between the woman and man, and I suddenly understood that the pin was probably much more valuable than the agreed-on price. Something my mother had told my father came back to me now. "Poor Cassandra is no businesswoman," my mother had said. "I think she just took over the shop after her father passed away because she hated working in the grocery store." She'd been a produce clerk at the local Giant food store.

At the time, I hadn't paid much attention to what she'd said. Now I understood. The woman probably didn't have a clue what the items in her shop were worth.

The couple left with their purchase. As they brushed past me, I overheard them gleefully planning a return visit.

I felt like warning Mrs. Hemingway, but why would she listen to me—the person the police believed had killed her niece?

"Hello," I said, when she looked up from some paperwork behind the cash register.

She stared at me as if she couldn't figure out whether or not she knew me.

"May I help you?" she asked.

"I just thought I . . ." I didn't know what to say. "I haven't seen you since Miranda . . ." My throat tightened on the words. I swallowed. "I'm sorry about what happened to her."

She narrowed her eyes at me. "Did you know Miranda?"

I nodded. "You probably don't recognize me. We

met at some of the ballroom competitions. Miranda and I both danced."

It seemed to take a while to sink in. "The competitions," she said slowly.

"I'm Carrie Clark. My brother Andy and I—"

"I know *you*!" she burst out. Her face reddened, and her spongy lips started trembling. "You were the awful girl who got Miranda so upset. She always had to dance against you. You did terrible things to beat her. She told me all about them."

My mouth dropped open. "*I* did terrible things to *her*?" I stammered over a couple of words, then finally came out with, "All I did was dance." How could I tell her that her dead niece hadn't played fair once in her life? That she'd have tried any trick, no matter how low, to win? You just don't talk like that about someone who's been murdered.

Cassandra Hemingway peered through thick lenses at me. "I think you'd better leave, young lady. The police told me what a troublemaker you are, breaking into my shop. You caused considerable damage!" she huffed. "I could press charges, you know."

This wasn't going well at all. "I thought someone had broken into your store again!" I protested. "I came over here because it might have been the person who'd killed Miranda!"

Her eyes narrowed to slits and she snorted. "I said, you'd better leave."

"Okay," I said apologetically. "I'm sorry I bothered you."

I turned to go. She came out from behind the counter and followed me toward the door. As we moved through the shop, my eyes wandered to the side room where the mermaid had fallen on me. I looked thankfully at the long work table that had bro-

122

ken its impact. In the light of day, the table looked different. Its surface was not only rough, it was speckled with an amazing variety of paint colors.

I stopped walking. "What is that table used for?" I asked.

"That's just a work area. You were leaving," Mrs. Hemingway reminded me sharply.

"Did Miranda use it?"

"I guess so, sometimes. For homework projects, I suspect."

I detoured across the room toward the table.

"Wait a minute!" the woman called after me. "I told you, you have to leave."

"I want to see something," I said, shutting out her protests.

When I'd stopped in front of the table, I ran my hand over its top. Blotches of color—muted earth tones, soft sky blues, vivid carnelian and subtle ocher decorated its bumpy surface in no particular pattern. It resembled an artist's pallet.

"Did the police see this?" I asked.

"They dusted all of the furniture for fingerprints." She was beginning to sound tired, as if putting up a tough front was a lot of work for her.

"I mean, did they look at this paint?"

"It's nothing. Just poster paints from school projects and campaign signs."

I remembered that Miranda had run for vice president of student counsel, and had won.

Something about what Isabelle had said, about Miranda not being very good at art, rang a bell. If she wasn't very good at it, why had she spent so much time messing around with paints? Campaign signs required only a couple of neon colors on cardboard. And never, in all the years I'd known Miranda, had I

123

seen her walk into school with a class project that was anything but store-bought.

"I want to scrape a little of this paint off for the police," I said.

Mrs. Hemingway threw up her hands and turned away. "I'm going to call the police right this minute. You shouldn't be here bothering me this way, you crazy girl." She took off, mumbling something to herself I couldn't catch.

I quickly scratched off a little of four or five colors from the table with my thumbnail and swept the shavings into a Kleenex. Folding it carefully, I tucked it into my purse.

I wasn't sure what the paint splotches meant, but something about them didn't make sense. And anything I could do to find Miranda's killer might help us find Andy.

"Don't you want to follow up on this?" I demanded.

I'd walked to the Baltimore County police station and found Red there. She'd looked at the little chips of paint I'd dumped on her desk, then at me with a hopeless expression.

"They might be important," I persisted.

She sighed. "I can send these samples for analysis, but I'm sure they've got nothing to do with Miranda Hemingway's death or your brother's disappearance. An antique store undoubtedly uses paint all the time, for refinishing furniture and touching up chipped picture frames and things like that."

"No," I said, still standing beside her desk. "I'm sure Mrs. Hemingway doesn't do any refinishing there. She doesn't even know enough about antiques to be able to sell them at a profit. And Miranda wasn't artistic at all."

I thought about Isabelle, who was a talented artist. If the police wouldn't look at the shavings, maybe Isabelle could tell me something about them—at least what kind of paint they were, and maybe even what it might have been used for.

"I'll see what I can do," Red agreed at last.

After watching her scoop the paint chips back into the tissue, I stared down at my empty hands. "No news about Andy?" I asked.

Her wide face seemed to soften. "I'm afraid not. We have a bulletin out on his car and on him. Something should turn up soon."

A chill passed through me, leaving me shaken, and I wrapped my arms around myself. I saw a flash of a lake being dragged and a car being pulled out of fifteen feet of water—a scene from a TV movie I'd watched a couple of weeks earlier.

I wondered if the police were thinking about doing things like that in their search for Andy. I wished those kinds of thoughts wouldn't keep popping into my head.

"Sit down, Carrie. You look tired," Red said, sounding concerned.

I looked at her. There was more than sympathy in her eyes, there was anticipation.

"If you think you can talk me into confessing to killing Miranda and my brother, you're crazy," I stated.

"No one's trying to talk you into anything," she assured me. "But you realize that this has all been very hard on your parents. Once this is over, no matter how bad it turns out, it will be better for them. They need to know what happened to their son."

"I need to know too! He's my brother." I choked out, tears filling my eyes.

"Well, yes," she said, looking away from me.

I knew she thought I was somehow involved. I expected my parents still figured I knew something about Miranda's death, but they also knew I'd never do anything to hurt Andy.

"Listen," I said, shakily, "I could never do the things you're accusing me of."

"No one's accusing you of anything," she repeated for the hundredth time, her eyes drilling into me.

Sure, I thought. *Tell me another one*.

"I've got to go," I mumbled.

"Remember, if you want to talk, I'm here," Red called out.

I walked home, although I was supposed to meet my father at the studio. I needed some time to pull myself together. I didn't know how my father was doing it, teaching dance classes, being polite and upbeat with students while Andy was still missing.

Maybe it was easier than sitting at home like my mother—waiting for the phone to ring, wondering if it would be the police with news that Andy's car had been found in some remote ditch, his body slumped over the steering wheel.

Stop it! I told myself. *Thinking like that is doing no one any good.* I walked into my bedroom and collapsed on my bed, pulling my stuffed monkey into the curl of my body, holding him close for warmth. How could my life have become such a mess?

A few minutes later the phone rang, jarring me out of a half-sleep. I wiped tears from my cheeks and coughed to clear my throat, before picking up the receiver. "Hello?"

There was no answer, but I could hear someone breathing at the other end.

"Who is this?" I demanded.

"Do you want your brother back?" a voice asked.

My fingers gripped the plastic receiver. My pulse throbbed in my forehead. "Of course," I said hoarsely.

There was a soft rustling sound in the background, then noise that sounded like traffic going by fast. *Whoosh, whoosh, whoosh*—tires singing on pavement, and the burst of a vacuum when something bigger, like a truck, passed by.

"Who is this? Are you a reporter? This is a sick—"

"If you want your brother back, you have to tell the police you killed Miranda Hemingway."

"What?" I couldn't have heard right. The voice was low—and it was impossible to tell if it was a man's or a woman's. The traffic sounds made it even harder to hear. "What about Miranda?"

"You killed her. Tell the police."

I bit down on my lower lip. "But I didn't—"

"If you don't tell them some time today that you did it, your brother will die."

"But I—"

The line went dead.

I stared in horror at the receiver, at first unable to think at all. Then the awful truth rushed through my mind. I'd just talked to Miranda's killer!

The caller had to be the person who'd murdered her. Otherwise, why would he or she want me to confess to something I hadn't done?

Andy, I thought. *Oh, Andy!* He was in the hands of a killer!

Fresh tears sprang to my eyes, but I dashed them

away with my hand. The good news was, if I was right about the caller, Andy was still alive. The killer had kidnapped him to use him to bargain with. On the other hand, why kidnap him then wait a whole day before calling? Was it just as possible that Andy was already dead, and the killer's promise was empty, a bluff?

I pushed myself up off of the bed, the receiver still in my hand, calling to me in that brain-dead female voice, "If you need assistance, hang up and dial the operator ... if you are trying to reach another party ..."

I jammed my finger down on the disconnect button and released it. The dial tone buzzed loudly in my ear. With shaking hands, I punched in the number I'd memorized and asked for Sergeant Landry.

"We'll try to keep this away from the papers as long as possible," Red told my parents grimly.

"No!" I objected. "Tell someone at the *Baltimore Sun*, and the radio stations too."

My mother and father stared at me as if I were no longer the daughter who'd grown up in their house.

"Carrie," my mother said weakly, "I will *never* believe you killed Miranda. Why are you making up this story?

"Are you taking the blame to get attention?" my father asked, looking confused.

"It wouldn't be the first time someone killed to get her name in the news." Toup said, nodding wisely. "Teenage girls can be very high-strung."

"I'm *not* doing anything for attention," I moaned, "I just want people to know I've confessed. I want you to tell the press." How else would the person who'd called me know I'd followed directions?

My father stared at me. "This doesn't make sense. You're not a killer." He sat down beside me in the interrogation room. "Where is Andy?" he asked.

They all looked at me. I felt like a bug, worse than a bug . . . a germ . . . a single-celled amoeba that can only exist by gobbling up other life forms and destroying them.

"I don't know," I said.

"You claim you killed Miranda," Red pointed out. "If that's true and her death and Andy's disappearance are connected, you can tell us what happened to your brother."

I looked across the table at her. *Funny,* I thought, *as long as I'd denied having anything to do with Miranda's death, she'd seemed absolutely sure I was her killer.* Now there was a hint of doubt in her voice, and I could see questions in her green eyes.

"Keep looking for him," I said stiffly. "I can't tell you where he is. I don't know."

I was past tears now. I sat there, sealing my fate as a tape recorder whirred, eating up my words. I'd refused to wait to talk to the police until my father got hold of his lawyer. It didn't matter. Nothing mattered except the hope of saving Andy.

There were hours more of questions after the lawyer came. The police wanted details, lots of details:

"How did you kill Miranda?"

"I hit her over the head." A safe answer, since the papers had reported her skull had been crushed.

"What did you hit her with?"

"I don't remember."

"You must. Was it a lamp? A bookend? A vase?"

"A lamp," I said to shut them up.

They wanted to know if we'd argued, if Miranda

had threatened me, if I'd intended to kill her or just hurt her. The questions went on and on until I no longer thought about what I was saying. The words just came out.

"That's enough," the lawyer said when I dropped my head onto my arms, too exhausted to talk any longer. "She's been through a lot. Let her rest for awhile."

He promised to get me out on bail in a few hours. He did, but I wasn't supposed to leave my house, except to go to school. I knew I couldn't go to classes, though. The school would be crawling with reporters. I sat staring at the phone in my bedroom, waiting for the call that would tell me Andy was safe.

I kept my promise, you creep, I thought. *Now keep yours.*

Night fell slowly, but the telephone didn't ring.

"Hey! Hey, Carrie!"

I opened my eyes.

The room was dark, the night wind blowing my pink curtains inward as if they were pastel jail bars, reaching for me. I sat up on the bed and wiped the crusty remainders of sleep from my eyes.

The voice had sounded as if it were right beside me, but no one was in the room. I glanced at the telephone. The receiver was sitting in its cradle.

Slowly, I pushed off of the bed and moved toward the window. Lifting the curtains aside, I looked down into our backyard. Six guys stood in the bushes, staring up at me. Joe was in the middle.

"What are you doing here?" I whispered.

"We've come to help you," Joe said.

"Go away. There's nothing you can do." I felt miserable and confused. What was I supposed to do now?

How long would I have to wait to hear about Andy?

"There is," he said. "You didn't kill anyone."

"I told the police I killed Miranda, and that's how it's going to stay."

Joe groaned. "Come down here."

"I can't leave the house."

"One of the guys thinks he spotted Andy's car. Do you want us to call the police and tell them?"

My mind raced. If the killer thought I'd contacted the police, he might think I'd told them about the telephone call and faking my confession—then Andy would be doomed.

"No!" I gasped. "I'm coming down."

I was already dressed, but I dragged a brush quickly through my hair and grabbed my purse. I didn't know what they did to people who ignored court orders. But I figured if anyone discovered I'd skipped out, chances were I'd be in a real jail cell soon.

The boys were waiting behind our garage.

"Where is Andy's car?"

"Behind the old Preakness Estate." The Maryland plantation had been turned into a museum years ago. It was open only during the summer.

"Let's go," I said.

We took two cars, Joe driving Matt and me in his. The other guys piled into Ralph Sanders' car. "Why do we have the whole team with us?" I asked.

"I just figured we don't know who or what we're dealing with. There's been talk about Baltimore gangs moving out into the 'burbs." He shrugged.

Gangs, I thought. But that didn't make sense. Nothing had been stolen from the antique store. And gang members usually left behind graffiti, marking their turf.

"The real reason we're here is we don't want Joe

getting himself beaten senseless," Matt said from the backseat. "We expect to win States this year, as long as he's in good health."

I tried to smile, but the muscles in my face didn't work. My head was pounding and I was sweating Niagara Falls, even though it was getting chilly out. I looked at the digital clock on the dashboard. It read 1:20 A.M.

"Matt and I spotted the car an hour ago," Joe explained.

"You didn't look inside to see if Andy was there?" I asked.

He glanced sideways at me. "We were going to, but got interrupted. The car's hidden in the edge of the woods, and a parks service guard was making his rounds. He obviously hasn't seen the car yet, but he might have spotted us if we hung around."

"What were you guys doing at the Preakness anyway?" I asked.

"Staking out a really rad place to stick our team banner," Matt explained solemnly.

Before a game, tradition demands the Mencken High team string the school banner from a really obvious place in town. Once, the football team hung it from the scaffolding in the Towsontowne Mall center court. No one has been able to figure out how they got it up there without a crane. Another time they draped it across the front of the courthouse. The courthouse guards pulled it down, but they had to use one of Baltimore Gas and Electric's cherry pickers to reach it.

"We wanted to try to put it across the front of the manor house. They light it up at night, and you can see it from I-95." Joe looked at me. "We were driving in the back way when Matt thought he saw an animal's eyes reflecting our headlights."

"Ralph thought it was a deer and wanted to chase it," Matt added.

"It was the reflectors on a car. The license plate was Andy's," Joe said gently.

I took a deep breath, feeling nauseous. After hearing of my confession to the police, the killer might have intentionally left the car with Andy in it, knowing he'd be found.

But what if we got to it and found Andy's body, not Andy alive?

I let out a soft whimper and clenched my hands tightly in my lap as Joe turned off his headlights and drove the last few yards toward a stand of pine trees in the dark.

"We can check it out for you," Joe said. "You don't have to get out of the car if you don't want to."

"Joe just thought you'd want to be here," Matt explained. "I'll wait with you in the car if you want."

"No," I choked out, "I have to see for myself."

Our car pulled to a stop, with Ralph's right behind it. It was completely dark here, no streetlights, no house lights. The big plantation house was a hulking shadow a few hundred feet away.

I opened the passenger door and climbed out.

Joe came around the front and took my hand. We walked through the tall, scratchy grass toward the woods. All I could see of the Escort was a reflection of the moon on its windshield.

One of the guys whispered to Joe, "I have a flashlight."

"If it's not one of those real bright torches, we might be able to use it," he said. Joe looked at me. "Let me check things out first."

"No," I repeated. "Whatever happened to Andy, I have to know."

He nodded grimly.

I stepped through a tangle of brush and at last reached the driver's door of the Escort. The boxy red car had been Andy's pride and joy. The guy with the flashlight pointed its beam through the window.

Peering through the glass, I could just make out Andy's bookbag on the passenger seat. A 7-Eleven coffee cup rested in the plastic holder near the stick shift. His vinyl carrying case for his CDs and tapes lay on the floor of the backseat.

Andy was not there.

"The trunk," Matt murmured. "We should look."

Joe turned to me. "Do you have a key?"

Andy and I kept spare keys for each of the family cars, in case one of us got locked out. But I'd never used his. "I think so," I said, fishing around in my purse.

I handed it to Joe. "You do it," I said, stepping back.

I wanted him to be the one to open the trunk, not because I was afraid to see what was inside—although I was. My nervousness had more to do with Andy's love of leaping around a corner to surprise me in the dark. One part of my brain knew that what was happening was serious, not a game. The other part insisted on dishing out the same old warning: *Andy's going to pop up and shout "Gotcha!" as soon as you open that trunk*!

I wished that would happen with all my soul. I wished it was all a stupid game and Andy would make like a jack-in-the-box.

I looked at Joe. His mouth tightened into a straight line as he slid the key into the lock and turned it. The latch opened with a loud clack, made louder by the absolute stillness of the night around us.

Slowly, the trunk lid rose on its heavy hinges. Joe lifted it further, while the boy with the flashlight directed a yellow beam into the black cavity.

I held my breath and forced my eyes to focus on the trunk's contents: a toolbox, a lug wrench, and a small plastic crate filled with odds and ends—maps, instant tire resealer, windshield washer fluid, rags.

No body.

I let out a long sigh of relief, but my disappointment at not finding Andy alive was so keen, it felt as if my emotions were razor-sharp blades, slashing through me from the inside out.

"Wait," Joe said, when his friend started to swing the flashlight away. "Point it down inside again."

The yellow glow fixed on a spot in the trunk. Joe took the light from the other guy's hand and moved it back and forth across the felt trunk liner. He held it on one spot, reaching in with his hand.

"What is it?" I asked tightly. All I could see was a darker area in the middle of the liner.

"I think it's blood," Joe said. "Dried blood."

14 *The night spun around me.* I reached out, grabbing hold of Joe's arm to stop myself from toppling over.

"It's not as bad as it might be," he whispered hoarsely in my ear. "At least he's not . . . there's still a *chance* he's alive."

"Whoever jumped him at the mall must have thrown him in the trunk. He was hurt, he was bleeding!" I sobbed, shrinking away from the car in horror. My mouth tasted sour and dry. A bloody shadow seemed to fall over the dark woods. I couldn't stop shaking.

"But he's not here," Joe repeated. "If he were dead, there'd be no reason not to leave his body in the trunk."

I looked up at him through my tears. As tall as I was, Joe was taller, a very unusual circumstance for me where boys were concerned. For some reason I found his height comforting.

He turned suddenly and whispered something to Matt, who rounded up the other guys and herded them back toward Ralph's car. A moment later they drove off, leaving Joe and me alone.

"Come on," he said. "Let's take one more look around for clues, then get out of here."

We searched inside the car and around it on the ground, but found nothing.

"But why *keep* him?" I asked as we climbed back into Joe's car. "Why not let Andy go?"

He frowned, concentrating on the narrow dirt road, driving with his lights off so we wouldn't be spotted. "For protection? Maybe as long as the killer has Andy, he's safe in some way we don't know yet. Or maybe it's a way of controlling you."

"Me? Why am *I* so important?"

"I don't know, and obviously the police don't either."

I cringed at the word *police*. "I guess I have to tell them about the car," I said, as we turned into York Road, then followed it across the Baltimore Beltway. The thought of making another confession to Red—this one true—that I'd disobeyed the court order by leaving my house, made my stomach start feeling queasy again.

"Why call them?" Joe asked. "Why not let them keep looking until they turn up the car themselves?"

I shook my head. "No. I can't do that. The Escort might have fingerprints or some evidence we didn't find that will help them find Andy."

"You're probably right," Joe agreed after a moment. "But you still don't need to stick your neck out. I can make an anonymous call, tip them off about the location of the car."

I smiled at him. "You'd do that for me?"

"Sure." He looked a little embarrassed, as if he'd been caught doing something heroic and it didn't fit his image. "Listen, it's no big deal."

My heart gave a little flutter, but I quickly got it

under control. The night wind gently rocked the car as we pulled up in the street behind my house.

"So what do I do now? I *have* to find Andy somehow."

Joe stared out through the windshield, looking as confused as I felt. "Maybe we have to rethink what's already happened. Go back to the beginning, to Miranda's murder. Or even further back, to the night someone broke into the dance studio."

"I've thought about all that until my head feels like it'll explode."

"Think some more. Are there any other dancers who'd want to waste Miranda?"

I shook my head. "Not really. There are two couples from Pennsylvania and one from New York who Andy and I compete against all the time, and Miranda danced against them too. But they aren't cutthroat competitors like Miranda was."

"What about in school? Did anyone there hate her enough to kill her?"

I sighed. "You know how she was. Lots of kids didn't like her. But I don't know of anyone who'd go as far as killing her."

"What about her family? A lot of murders are committed by members of the victim's own family."

"She's the only child in her family, and her parents spoiled her rotten. I don't know of any cousins. Mrs. Hemingway, who owns the antique shop, is Miranda's father's sister. She's not married and doesn't have any kids."

Joe shook his head. "What about that brush you said you'd found?"

"That's a dead end so far. It's the one thing that doesn't seem to fit. I talked to Isabelle Vane, a girl I know from school who's into art in a super-big way.

She didn't know what it was for. She didn't think Miranda would have known what to do with a brush like that, and Miranda's aunt isn't at all handy or artsy.''

I frowned, remembering something Isabelle had said. "I think I'll try to find Tammy tomorrow and talk with her.''

"What's she got to do with all this?''

"I don't know, maybe nothing.'' But just bringing up her name made me start to wonder about her again. "The thing is, Isabelle mentioned how odd Tammy's been acting lately, and I think she's right. There's something strange going on with her.'' I shrugged. "I don't know . . . maybe it's nothing.''

"But if it isn't, you might be in danger, meeting alone with her.'' He studied my face, and the way he looked at me made me feel warm and safe. "I'm not sure I remember Tammy, but isn't she that girl you hang out with—the one that's sort of wound up too tight?''

"That's her—she changes moods every other hour.''

"Does she have anything against you or your family?''

I looked at him, shocked. "Not that I know of.''

He nodded. "Okay, you'd better get inside before someone sees you outside of your house.''

"You mean, in addition to you and your whole team?'' I smiled.

"Yeah.''

I started to slide out of the car. But Joe's hand reached out and touched me on the back of the neck. "Wait,'' he said softly.

I turned, expecting him to say something more

about Tammy or Andy, but he leaned across the seat and brushed his lips over mine.

I didn't pull away. He kissed me a little longer, and I felt even warmer inside. Although he hadn't said a word, it seemed as if things might still turn out okay.

"Good night," I whispered.

" 'Night," he said.

The next morning my father woke me up by pounding on my bedroom door loud enough to wake a hibernating bear.

"The police have found Andy's car," he said, watching my face closely as he stood in the doorway. "He wasn't in it."

I nodded, not able to trust myself to talk. I didn't want to lie anymore; it was better if I said nothing at all.

"Your mother is pretty upset," he added. "I don't suppose you have anything more to tell the police."

"No," I said.

He looked at me for a long moment, opened his mouth, then closed it without saying the words that were too difficult for him to get out.

"I would never do anything to hurt Andy," I told him for what seemed like the fourth time. "You have to believe me, Dad."

He nodded. "I know that, Carrie. I just don't understand what's going on. I wish you could tell me the truth." With a last puzzled look at me, he turned away and closed the door behind him.

I sat on my bed, listening to his footsteps fade down the hallway, feeling awful because everything was such a mess and Dad was trying not to think badly of me, even though I'd told the world I'd killed a girl.

My mother didn't come out of her room all morning. The police must have told her about the blood in the trunk. *This whole thing stinks, it really stinks,* I thought. *If I ever find out who's behind this, maybe I really will kill someone.*

When I finally went downstairs that afternoon, my father looked as if he'd have liked to shut himself up in the house too, just to get away from people and their questions. But he said he had to open the studio and give lessons that afternoon and evening. I figured he was worried about how he was going to pay for the lawyer. My defense lawyer.

"Maybe it's better he keeps busy," I told Diana when she brought me my assignments later that day. "I wish my mother would do the same. She's still in her room, crying."

"She's probably already mourning Andy," Diana said sadly.

At the word *mourning*, a tear I hadn't felt coming slid down my cheek. I licked it away with the tip of my tongue. The salt made me think of the ocean. Andy loved the ocean. Andy might never see the ocean again.

My eyes dropped to the black vinyl binder in Diana's arms. "What's that?"

She glanced down at it. "Student council minutes, and the class ring orders. You already put down your deposit, right?"

I nodded without enthusiasm. "Somehow, getting my ring doesn't seem as important now as it did last month."

"The girl's style this year is beautiful." Diana was obviously trying to cheer me up. "Especially in the eighteen-carat gold. A couple of them came with the last order, even though most kids buy the ten-carat setting. It's like half the price."

141

Something jangled in my mind. "Do you know which students ordered the more expensive ones?"

"Sure, everything's on the order forms. I always keep a copy, in case someone forgets what they ordered. Why?"

"I just . . . I'm not sure. Let me see them."

Diana handed me the ring portfolio. I flipped it open and ran a finger down the list, looking for one name.

"Who are you trying to find?"

"Tammy. I want to know if she got real gold."

"You're crazy. She can't afford one of those rings. They're almost four hundred dollars!"

But she had been acting very strange, Isabelle was right. Maybe there was a very simple motive for killing Miranda that no one had thought of—like money. Tammy was always fantasizing about getting rich and helping out her mother by paying off some loans.

My mind whirled with wild, unconnected theories. None of them made much sense, yet. But with another look at the evidence from a different angle—they might!

I found Tammy's name at the top of an order sheet. Beside it, in the first block, was a black check mark. She'd ordered the least expensive ring, with a glass stone instead of the more costly garnet or topaz. It hadn't come in yet.

I sighed.

"Satisfied?" Diana asked, looking disgusted with me. "You've known Tammy too long to think she could actually hurt anyone. You should be ashamed of yourself."

"Yeah." I nodded. "I guess I'm just desperate."

I'd already told her about the threatening phone call, the reason why I'd confessed to the police when

I had nothing to confess. Now I filled her in on Andy's car, and what we'd found in it.

"I'm sorry," she said, avoiding my eyes the way people do in a funeral parlor when they're standing over the casket. There was nothing she could say to make me feel better.

"Thanks."

I'd started to close the portfolio, when my eye settled on another check mark on the far right-hand side of the page, one of the few in that column. I read the caption at the top: *18 c./deluxe setting.*

My eyes skimmed back to the left side, and the name of the student.

Isabelle Vane.

"She lied to me!" I gasped.

"Who? What?" Diana demanded.

"Isabelle. I saw her ring and told her how beautiful it was. I thought it looked more expensive than the one I'd chosen, but she said it wasn't." I looked up at Diana. "Why do you suppose she lied to me?"

"I don't know." She studied the order page, as if to reassure herself she hadn't made a mistake in her records. "I remember taking her order in the cafeteria. It was so busy that day at lunchtime, I didn't even think about it. But now that you mention it, I would never have thought she could afford a ring like that. And look here! She paid in full—cash."

"I see it," I murmured, and wondered if our discovery meant something . . . or nothing at all.

As soon as Diana left, I called Joe.

"Get over here fast," I said. "Something's happened."

"Right." In what seemed like less than two

minutes, he was running up the driveway to our front door.

I let him inside.

"What is it?" he gasped, out of breath.

"Just come in," I said. As soon as he was through the door, I carefully pulled aside one edge of the living room curtains and peeked out. "See that brown car over there?"

"Yeah," he said. "Ugly, isn't it?"

"I think it's an unmarked police car. It was there last night after I got home from going to the plantation, and it has been sitting there all day. The driver hasn't moved and he keeps looking this way."

Joe frowned at the car. "They're making sure you stay home?"

"I guess."

He nodded. "Is that why you called me over here?"

"No, I need to drive to Annapolis."

"Why?"

"I found out that Isabelle Vane lied to me about her class ring."

He laughed. "What?"

"I'm serious, this might really be important. Isabelle told me her ring was the cheap kind, but it's eighteen-carat gold."

"Didn't you tell me she was selling her paintings to a dealer?"

"Yeah, and she could have earned the money that way. But why lie to me, unless she's trying to cover something up?"

Joe glanced out the window. "My car's out front. No way can you get to it without your shadow seeing you."

"Bring it around to the street behind, like we did last night. I'll tell my mother I'm going to be in my room cramming for a test, so she won't bother me."

"See you," Joe said, and walked out the front door.

I went upstairs and tapped on my mother's bedroom door. "You okay, Mom?"

"Yes," she answered softly.

I felt awful for her, for all of us. But there wasn't anything more I could do than what I was doing now. "I'm not going to answer the phone or anything for a few hours. I'm studying for a test, okay?"

"Fine," she murmured.

I figured she was probably going back to sleep. When she got worried, she slept a lot. People like Tammy eat tons of junk food when they're upset. Others drink or do drugs. I bite my nails. My mother sleeps.

Maybe this will all have gone away by the time I wake up! That's probably what she was thinking.

I looked out the kitchen door. It was possible the police had put someone out back, but I suspected I wasn't that high of a priority. Why waste two cops for every shift when one would probably do?

Joe was waiting in front of a brick house a lot like ours, with the motor running.

"Take the Beltway, then I-97 south. It's the fastest way to Annapolis," I said.

"Right."

There was no traffic, but the ride took forty minutes anyway. We stopped at a pay phone so I could look up the addresses of art galleries in the phone book. Most were located near the city marina, in the tourist district.

"I don't know which dealer she's selling to, but the owner should know her by name," I said.

"Maybe telephoning around would save time."

145

"Good idea." I was glad we were working together. I could have blown hours of valuable time if I'd tried going door to door for all of them. "We'll eliminate the galleries by the docks first, since we're here. Then we can start calling the others."

As it turned out, we hit pay dirt at the third shop we visited.

"Yes, of course I know Isabelle," a plump woman in an African print caftan said when I asked about her. "She's brought us some lovely work."

I shot a look of triumph at Joe. "May we see it?"

The woman floated ahead of us, through a front room that displayed mostly seascapes and local landscapes. In the second room were displays in an African motif that matched her outfit. In a third, many different kinds of paintings lined the walls, and they had a more subdued feeling to them.

"There," she said, extending an open hand to a row of landscapes on one wall. "Those are three of the paintings Isabelle brought to me most recently."

I stared at them, surprised.

Joe stepped closer and squinted at the signature. "That's not her name. It says Edwin Walters."

The woman laughed. "Of course it does. Walters was the artist who painted that one."

"Isabelle didn't paint any of these?" I asked.

"Oh my dear, no!" she tittered. "These are all lovely oils done over two hundred years ago. Miss Vane works for a gallery in Baltimore, you see. They're trying to unload some of their estate stock. They're short on display space and she's bringing some pieces for me to sell on consignment. I must say, they've gone quite quickly so far."

I turned to Joe. "I was sure she told me the paintings she was selling, *she* painted," I whispered.

"Is something wrong?" the woman asked.

"No. At least, I'm not sure," I said, puzzled. Had I misunderstood Isabelle? Or was it possible that she had indeed painted these? Was she involved in art forgery?

"I have a question," I said cautiously.

"Yes?"

"If these were *copies* of old paintings instead of originals, would you know it?"

The woman looked surprised. "I should hope so! I could lose a lot of money and customers by selling forged art."

The gallery owner didn't look nearly as cheerful now. She glanced at the first painting—a barn and a mowed field in the distance, snow encrusting stark, black tree branches in the foreground. The picture was pretty in a very simple way.

She touched the surface of the canvas. "You aren't saying that you think—"

"Oh no," I fibbed. "I'm sure these are the real thing. I've just got this report I have to write for art class, and I thought forgeries might be an interesting topic."

The owner let out a long breath. "Thank goodness." She pressed a hand to her chest. I hoped she wasn't going to have a heart attack.

"What would you look for to be sure a painting was real?" I asked.

"Well..." She stepped forward. "Not all copies of paintings were meant to be illegal forgeries. Art students often copy masters' paintings to study their technique. But they generally use modern canvases. A new canvas dates the work as a copy. However, if a forger wants to fool prospective buyers or even experts, he'll use old canvas, from the time of the original artist."

"You can get that?" I asked. "Canvases hundreds of years old?"

"Oh, quite easily. If I wanted to, I could order used eighteenth-century canvas scraps from a European dealer, then paint over them. The backs would look quite authentic." She studied the snowy field of the landscape in front of her. "But I would suspect the painting if I saw parts of other paintings beneath it. Walters, for instance, always painted on new canvas."

"How else would you know?" I asked.

She walked over to a desk and plucked a common pin out of a glass ashtray holding paper clips, pins, and thumbtacks. Aiming at a section of paint that represented snow, she jabbed the pin at the canvas.

"See?" she said.

I looked closely at the painting. "I can't see anything."

"Exactly. The paint is very hard, two-hundred-years hard. The pin won't go into it unless I really push."

"So," Joe said, "if this were a fake, you could make a pin prick in it?"

"Easily," she said. "The pin would leave a tiny mark in the soft pigment. It's especially easy to detect in white paint."

"Well, what do you think?" Joe asked, when we'd stepped out onto the sidewalk.

"I don't know now. I thought Isabelle was copying paintings and selling the forgeries to galleries in Annapolis, but they're the real thing."

"Maybe she was stealing them from Mrs. Hemingway, and Miranda found out," he suggested.

I rubbed my forehead; it was starting to ache. "Cassandra Hemingway may be kind of dim, but she's not totally stupid. Don't you think she'd notice if paintings started disappearing from her walls? No, Isabelle must be getting them from somewhere else."

"Where?" he asked. "And why does this have anything to do with Miranda or Andy?"

"Maybe it has nothing to do with them," I admitted, discouraged with the outcome of the day. "Maybe we're wasting time bothering with Isabelle. But she's all we've got, so far."

15 I couldn't stay home and listen to the silence in the house. I didn't know what to say to my mother anymore.

It's okay, Mom. You still have me. We'll get over losing Andy . . . someday.

That was so lame.

I called my father at the studio. "Please, can I come down there with you?"

"I don't know," he said cautiously. "The judge was pretty specific about your being either in the house or at school."

I couldn't tell him I'd been from one end to the other of two counties in the last twenty-four hours. "I promise I'll come straight there. I'll be with *you*, Dad. What trouble can I get into?"

"All right," he agreed at last.

I could hear students' voices in the background. He was in the middle of a class and in a hurry to get off the phone. Knowing him, he'd probably signed up extra students and agreed to teach later than usual, just to keep his mind off of what was happening.

"Come straight here," he said before hanging up. "No stops along the way."

Like I'd drop in at a friend's house and party for a

couple of hours, while a police stakeout sat outside and the rest of the force searched for my brother's body.

I left a note for my mother on the fridge, in case she came out of her room to look for me. Throwing on my suede jacket and grabbing my purse, I stepped out of the front door and looked around. The unmarked car was nowhere in sight. Had they stopped watching me? That didn't make sense, unless something about their investigation had changed.

I jogged through the already darkening streets for the first half mile, feeling panic rise inside of me. Maybe something had happened—maybe they'd found Andy . . . or what had been Andy . . .

When I couldn't run any farther, I walked in long, hurried strides, my head down, shoulders hunched over, thinking about Isabelle and Miranda and Andy and me. What truth kept escaping me that tied us all together? I had a feeling that if my head were clear, if I weren't so scared about Andy and worried about my parents and terrified I was going to spend the rest of my life in jail, I'd be able to figure all of this out.

The way to the studio came automatically to me, I didn't have to think about which corner to turn or how far to go down the next block. My thoughts were jumbled and black, and spiraled off into nowhere.

It started to rain. Cars sizzled down the damp roads.

I was somewhere on Court Street when I sensed I was no longer alone. A soft sound, like the echo of my own footsteps, trailed after me. I stopped and listened, breathing hard. I took a step and then another, but heard nothing.

Then the echo started again, and I thought it might be the sound of my own steps bouncing crazily off the city buildings. After I'd turned the corner onto

151

Allegheny, I intentionally stopped short. Three distinct footfalls grated against the pavement after mine had ceased.

I turned around and looked up the street. An old woman wearing a coat several sizes too big for her and a bulky knit cap pulled down over her head was hobbling along the sidewalk a ways down. She gazed idly at the display windows of Miller Brothers' Furs of Distinction. They probably wouldn't have waited on her if she dared step inside.

At the far end of the street a group of college students hung out outside of Strapazzi's Pizza. No one seemed close enough to have made the footsteps I'd heard.

Quickly, I ran the rest of the way to the door of Dying to Dance, and ducked into the vestibule. I shot a longing look at the elevator but opted for the stairs for speed.

I ran up all three flights and shot out of the door, into the upstairs hallway. Bill Haley singing "Rock Around the Clock" greeted me. The voices of students, laughing at something going on during their class, suddenly made my fear seem silly.

Still I went to the window and looked down into the street.

The old woman had moved down several stores but seemed in no hurry to go anywhere in particular. She looked as if she couldn't have moved very fast if she'd wanted to.

I thought about warning her she'd better go home, wherever that was. Towson wasn't what you'd call a mecca of crime, but every once in a while some slime-bucket jumped a senior citizen for his or her social security money. Old people seemed to like to carry cash, and the wrong people always knew it.

She'll be okay, I tried to reason with myself. I was feeling vulnerable and wanted to protect myself more than anyone else. Besides, I had my own family to worry about.

"Carrie."

I turned away from the window.

"Is anything wrong?" my father asked. He wore his usual, neatly pressed white dress shirt and dark pants with a conservative necktie. But his eyes looked old, drained of energy.

"No, I was just . . ." I blinked, swallowing, wishing he'd smile at me the way he used to.

Behind him stood his class. I'd forgotten, it was Wedding Survival night again. Joe was there with eight other students. *Great*, I thought. *Just what I need*.

"Nothing," I murmured. "It's nothing."

"We're short one lady," my father said. "Come join us for the rest of the hour."

I nodded. It was better to keep busy than let my brain run in circles the way it had been doing lately. Andy . . . Isabelle . . . Mrs. Hemingway . . . Miranda . . . me. Maybe someone else I hadn't even thought about was involved—like Tammy or Diana or some of Joe's crazy friends! Somehow I had to figure out the missing connections.

"We're working on swing tonight," Dad interrupted my dismally whirling thoughts. "Mr. Frances needs a partner, Carrie."

Mr. Frances must have weighed three hundred pounds if he weighed an ounce. He had greasy gray hair and feet that plopped heavily with every step he took—not my idea of an ideal dance partner. But he could keep time with the music, and he didn't step on my foot once.

153

We switched partners several times, practicing basic steps my father had already introduced. At last I ended up with Joe.

"Are you okay?" he asked.

I shrugged.

"I stopped in at Strapazzi's for supper," he commented as the music started up again. We bounced to the beat of Bette Midler's version of the thirties swing tune "Boogie Woogie Bugle Boy." Joe led me into a throwaway and underarm turn. Not bad at all.

"So?" I prompted.

"I saw Tammy and Diana there."

There was something serious on his mind, I could see it in his eyes. "What?"

"Tammy was acting weird. She saw me, but when I waved to her she just turned away, pretended not to recognize me."

"That's odd. What about Diana?"

"I don't think she ever saw me. They were arriving just as I was leaving."

"Maybe Tammy really didn't recognize you."

"Maybe. I don't know, I just get the funniest feeling about that girl. It's as if she's hiding something."

Joe led me into an American spin, and I looked up at him, for a moment my mind on something other than murder and kidnapping. "Hey, that was pretty good. When did you learn that?"

"Tonight, right after I got here." He blushed, looking pleased. "I was watching a man and woman from an advanced class practice. It looked like fun, and I thought I could probably lead it."

"You did great. Try again."

He did, and I was amazed, but also a little irritated. After the lecture I'd given him the other day about it taking years of practice to be any good at dancing,

154

here he was ad-libbing difficult steps and making them look easy.

We finished the class, and Joe hung around while the other students wandered into the foyer by my mother's desk. It looked lonely, sitting there without her, with only the answering machine to pick up calls. My father made a show of cheerfully sending everyone off for the night, reminding them of the date of their next class, encouraging them to invite their friends to join up, or just come along with them to watch.

I picked up used paper cups around the water fountain, closed the miniblinds on the row of windows, and shut off the lights in the two practice rooms. Joe followed me around, silently helping even though I hadn't asked him to.

At last it was just the three of us.

"Ready to leave, Carrie?" my father asked.

Joe stepped forward. "Actually, sir, I was wondering if Carrie could help me out. I'd like to practice for just a little while."

"She's supposed to be at home when she's not in school or here with me or her mother," my father said tiredly.

"Dad," I pointed out, "the studio is *just like* home. It really is. I'll be fine here. And if the police need me, you can tell them where I am."

He looked too exhausted to argue. "All right, but don't stay long." He turned to Joe. "Do you have a car?"

"Yes, sir."

"Drive her home. She's not to walk alone tonight. And I want her there by eleven, no later."

"Yes, sir," Joe said, straightening up, as if he were a military cadet, snapping to attention.

"See you in an hour," Dad said, and kissed me on the forehead.

I waited for him to leave before moving. Then all I could do was drop my gaze to the floor and swallow all of the awful sadness and shame.

Joe put an arm around me. "He's nice. I like him."

"Me too," I choked out.

"Well," Joe said, "let's make the most of our dance time." He let his arm slip away from my waist, marched toward the tape deck, then started flipping through stacks of cassettes.

"You were serious about dancing?" I asked, astonished.

"Of course I was." He turned and grinned at me. "How am I going to get ready for the Mid-Atlantics if we don't practice?"

Now I knew he was putting me on. "Oh, right," I groaned. "Like that's a serious possibility."

"*I'm* taking it seriously," he said. "I don't know why you won't."

I stared at him. "You can't possibly learn to dance on a competitive level in only a few weeks."

"I'd never played tennis until my sophomore year. I decided to take it up, since I'd played every other sport and made varsity in most of them." He observed me solemnly, his brown hair slipping down over one bright blue eye. "I was ranked fourth of all Maryland amateurs this year."

"But what about your friends? They'll never let you forget it if they find out what you're doing."

"No one bothers Andy anymore. Maybe they won't make a big deal about it for me, either. Besides, I've decided you were right. What they say doesn't matter. You show me the moves, I'll do 'em."

I laughed. "You're crazy, Joe! It won't work." He

was probably just making all of this up to take my mind off of everything else.

"You won't know until you try," he said. "Never, never, never, never give up."

I blinked at him. He was trying to tell me something and it wasn't about dancing.

Maybe, like my mother, I'd started to give up on ever finding my brother.

"You know who said that?" Joe asked.

I grinned, and reached up to put my arms around his wide neck. *Never, never, never, never give up!* "You did."

"Nope. Winston Churchill, Prime Minister of England during World War II. He was famous for not giving up."

I took a deep breath. And he'd had Hitler to worry about. "Let's dance," I said.

We worked on the waltz and the quickstep, two very difficult dances in the modern category. Joe was a natural in the waltz. His long legs ate up yards of wooden floor, and the body sway that comes from years of practice seemed easy for him. "Just like faking a move on the basketball court," he said as we veered from one corner of the room to the other.

The quickstep was harder for him. It required very fast footwork, coordinated perfectly between the two partners. If we were doing a turn and he stepped outside one of my feet when he was supposed to come down between them, we'd end up crashing to the floor.

And we did. More than once.

But dancing with a goal left me breathless, tingling, and feeling alive again.

I wished Andy had been there to see us. He would

have cracked up laughing. He also would have applauded when we finally succeeded in getting through a sequence of steps without slamming into the mirror, a chair, or each other.

We'd been working for quite a while when the phone rang and I automatically looked at the clock. Joe followed my glance.

"Oh great, it's five after eleven . . . and I promised your dad I'd have you home by now!" He grabbed the towel I'd brought out earlier and blotted his face with it. "Tell him we're on the way."

"All right," I said, running for the desk.

I picked up and opened my mouth to reassure my father, but a hysterical, high-pitched voice shrieked at me. "I gave you a chance to save your brother! I gave you a chance!"

"Who is this?" I demanded.

"Who do you *think* it is? I told you I'd let him go if you did what I asked. I told you to quit snooping around!"

"You told me to tell the police I'd killed Miranda and to not tell them about your phone call. I followed your directions."

"Liar!" the voice screamed. "You and your friends snooped around and found the car."

"But I didn't tell the cops about the car." That much was the truth. Joe had done it for me. "I swear, I didn't tell them anything about it."

A sobbing sound came through the line, slowly fading and becoming less frantic. It sounded like a woman's voice, but it still could have been a guy, pretending. Behind the muffled crying, I could almost hear the person thinking, trying to figure out what to do next. I waved at Joe, motioning for him to come over to the phone.

"I'll give you one more chance to help me and save your brother," the caller said.

Joe walked toward me, a questioning look on his face. Putting a finger to my lips, I held the receiver so he could hear too. I had a feeling the caller would hang up if he or she knew someone else was listening in.

"All right. I promise I'll do what you say," I said.

"I need money—at least a thousand dollars. I have to get away from here."

"I don't have that kind of money. There's less than five hundred dollars in my savings account." My costume fund.

"You have a friend. She orders class rings."

"Yes," I said slowly, glancing at Joe, who looked puzzled.

"She takes cash sometimes, for deposits and payments?"

I shook my head, thinking about Diana. Giving me that money would be like stealing it from the kids who'd trusted her to pay the ring company.

"Doesn't she keep the money?" the voice persisted impatiently.

"Yes, until she places the order. But I . . ." My mind was racing. *Whoever this is must be from Mencken High,* I thought. He or she knew me and my friends very well. If I asked Diana to give me the money and make up a lie about it having been stolen, she'd probably do it for me. It was an awful thing to ask of her, though. "I'll talk to her," I said.

"I need the money tonight."

"But I—"

"*Tonight*, and your brother goes free. If I don't get it, I have no choice. He'll die."

159

"Why?" I cried. "He hasn't done anything to you!"

"Meet me outside the high school, behind the field house at 3:00 A.M.," the voice instructed. "Remember, this is your last chance. I need that money."

The line went dead.

I stared at Joe. "Andy's alive!"

It struck me as glorious news at that moment. It had to be true, there was no other explanation for the conversation I'd just had.

But Joe's eyes darkened, and the muscles in his neck tightened. "How do you know he's alive?

"Andy must be alive. That person was too upset to have already killed him. She doesn't want to do it. He must know her. He must be conscious and have seen her face! That's why she needs the money, to get away from here so when he's freed and he identifies her, she'll be out of reach of the police."

I grabbed Joe by the arms and shook him, feeling happier than I'd ever felt. Happier than I'd be if I ever won the Nationals.

Andy was alive!

Joe didn't smile. "I hope you're right," he murmured. "What do you want to do?"

"Get the money." And I told him how it had to happen.

16

``I've saved up almost five hundred dollars for costumes and other expenses for comps,'' I explained. ``I can get it out with my ATM card.''

``And the rest? She said she needed a thousand.''

This part didn't sit well with me. I'd thought and I'd thought, but I couldn't come up with any other solution. ``Diana, she keeps the class ring money. There's no other way on such short notice. I can't go to my parents for the money— they'd call the police and ruin everything.''

``But what if there isn't enough? Or what if Diana won't give you any money?''

``She will. Diana would do anything for me, especially when she hears what I have to tell her.'' I sighed. ``If we're just a hundred or two short, it will be okay. I know Tammy. She won't count the money.''

``What's Tammy got to do with this?'' Joe looked totally lost.

I couldn't blame him. Only a minute ago, the truth had finally struck me. ``I don't know what happened to Miranda that night, not exactly. But I think Tammy has Andy. I'm almost certain she's the person who just called me."

"You recognized her voice?"

"I recognized her typical hysteria. She goes off the deep end sometimes, like when she's on a sugar high or diet low. Besides, how many kidnappers would call their victim's sister in tears and ask for only a thousand dollars, hoping they wouldn't have to kill him?"

Joe nodded. "You're right. Pros would pick someone whose family was rich. And there'd be no big guilt trip if they had to waste him."

"Exactly." I watched the buildings flash past us in the dark. Joe was driving south toward the downtown area.

He scowled at the road. "I don't know. Why Tammy? Why would she kill Miranda?"

"Because Miranda was so mean to me." He didn't know Miranda or Tammy the way I did. "Tammy used to get furious when Miranda pulled mean stunts on me at the comps. Sometimes she'd work herself into a terrible mood, and she'd brood and brood and brood about things.

"The girl on the phone said she has to get out of here. I'll bet Tammy and Miranda had a fight and there was an accident and . . ." It must have been terrible for Tammy, realizing she'd killed someone. She couldn't have meant to do it. "Maybe Tammy thought it would all blow over, but then the police suspected me and I started nosing around and—"

"Wait a minute," Joe interrupted. "You're forgetting one thing. Whoever is behind this *intentionally* framed you. Remember the bracelet? That was left in the mall parking lot to make it look like you'd had something to do with Andy's disappearance. And before that, there was your dress." He turned a corner a little too fast; and the tires squealed.

He slowed down, muttering under his breath.

"You're right," I said slowly. "I can see Tammy doing something crazy without thinking about the consequences. But fixing evidence so it would look like I'd killed Miranda or kidnapped Andy doesn't sound like her." I thought for a minute, rubbing my throbbing shoulder. My head ached too from thinking so hard. Why wasn't this making sense, even now? "Maybe someone else was trying to frame me. Maybe Tammy had nothing to do with that part."

We drove up to the automatic teller at Maryland National Bank, a few blocks from the studio. I used my card to take out all of my savings. I wished the machine could have given it to me in tens. The twenties didn't make much in a stack. What if Diana didn't have the ring money at home with her? I'd have to make it look as if there was more cash than I really had.

I called Diana from a pay phone near the bank.

"I know it's late, but I'm coming over," I said. "It's important."

"Is it about Andy?" she whispered, sounding as if she were ready to cry if the news turned out bad.

"I'll explain when I get there."

Joe stayed in the car while I ran to Diana's kitchen door. She was waiting for me.

"What's happened?" she asked breathlessly, pulling me into her mother's cheery red-and-white kitchen.

"The person who has Andy contacted me," I said, choosing my words carefully. "I think it's a girl, someone we know. She wants a thousand dollars."

Diana stared at me. "What are you going to do?"

163

I told her about my five hundred.

"So you want me to put up the rest," she guessed immediately. Diana's no dummy. "You know I don't have any money of my own. It's all for class rings."

"I know. I promise, once Andy's safe, I'll work my butt off to pay back every penny. This is my last chance. I can't let Andy be hurt any more than he already has been. I can't let her kill him."

"Her?" Diana said, squinting at me. "You keep saying it's a her, and someone we know. Who is it?"

I had no idea how she'd take the news, or if she'd even believe me. But I owed her an explanation.

I touched her arm and looked at her sadly. "The kidnapper is T—"

"What's all the noise about?" someone called from the next room.

Diana rolled her eyes at the interruption "Never mind her. Go on, who is it?"

I stared at the doorway, a shudder rising from the tips of my toes, snaking through my body. *No!* I thought. *It can't be!*

Charging across the kitchen, I pushed open the door to the family room. The TV was on, showing a movie I didn't recognize. On the other side of the dark room sat a sofa bed, pulled out and made up with sheets. A sleeping bag lay on the floor between the sofa and the TV.

Tammy blinked at me from the folds of plaid flannel. "Carrie? Are you going to sleep over too?"

Joe was waiting for me in the car. I threw myself into the passenger seat and shouted, "Drive!"

"The school?" he asked.

"Yeah, I guess . . . I don't know. This is terrible."

I pressed my face into my hands, wishing I understood what was going on.

"What's wrong now?" he asked.

"It's not Tammy," I said through a bone-dry throat. "She's been with Diana all night. They've been watching videos for the last three hours."

"Would Diana—"

"Why would she trick me into coming to *her* for money? That doesn't make sense. She couldn't be in on it."

"I guess not," Joe agreed.

At the school, we parked within sight of the field house. Joe cut the car's engine and we sat, peering into the dark.

On any Saturday afternoon in the fall, the place had a totally different feeling. It was alive with crowds of students and parents, come to watch Mencken High play football. The plywood awnings of the concession stand on the other side of the field house would be raised. Student council members sold hotdogs, sodas, popcorn, and cups of steaming coffee and cocoa to the fans.

Win or lose, everyone had a great time at the game.

When it came right down to it, though, that was all it was . . . *a game!* Cheerleaders and fans might go home hoarse from screaming. A couple of players might leave the field with bruised ribs, black eyes, or an occasional fractured arm. But no one *died*.

No one ever died . . .

I swallowed and looked at Joe, thinking, *this is* not *a game. This is real.*

I was terrified.

Joe's expression was taut, and the skin at one corner of his mouth twitched nervously. "Maybe this isn't such a good idea," he said in a quiet voice. "Maybe we should go tell the police after all."

My stomach felt as if it were on fire, and my hands were damp with sweat. "No, we can't do that. If whoever was on the phone really meant what she said, she'll kill Andy if I don't show up. She knew about the police finding the car, and she was freaked out about it, thinking I'd called them."

Joe turned in the seat, one hand on the steering wheel, and reached out with his other toward me. He touched a fingertip gently to my lips. "It's dangerous. I don't want anything to happen to you."

"Andy's my brother." I swallowed. "I have to do this for him."

He nodded, as if he understood, even if he didn't agree with my decision. "What do you want me to do?"

"Just sit here and stay out of sight so you don't spook her. I don't know where on the field she'll be waiting, but I'll try to get her to move over this way so you can see what's happening."

I started to get out of the car. Joe's hand gently touched my shoulder. "You have no guarantee he's alive."

"I know," I said, tears filling my eyes. Then I gritted my teeth in determination and held up the stack of bills. "But she's not going to get this until I see him."

"How will you manage that?"

"I'll think of something," I said. "Promise you won't leave the car unless I call you?"

"Promise," he agreed reluctantly, sliding down in the seat so his head wouldn't be visible from the outside.

I climbed out and quietly closed the door. The air

felt bitter and moist, threatening snow although there were no clouds. The stars shone like brilliant white diamonds against an obsidian sky. It would have been a pretty night for anything except what I had to do.

Slowly, I crossed the gravel parking area then turned to the right and cut behind the field house. On the other side, I knew, was the football field, surrounded by a regulation quarter-mile cinder track. But back where I walked there was only overgrown grass and a few acres of woods.

A sudden motion caught my eye from within the trees, and I stopped, holding my breath . . . waiting. But no one stepped out from the trees. *Joe*, I thought grimly, *I told you to stay in the car.*

Drawing a deep breath, I moved on. If it was Joe, it wouldn't do any good to yell at him to go back. That would just tell the kidnapper someone had come with me, and she might think it was the police.

I circled once around the field house then leaned against it, waiting, breathing in the crisp air, blowing out a long puff of foggy breath, while my heart hammered inside my chest. I tried not to let my fear show in my face. If the person I'd come to meet was still in panic mode when she got here, I might have a small advantage . . . if I stayed in control.

A branch snapped behind me and I spun around.

A figure emerged, like a ghost from a grave, from behind the corner of the gray-painted field house. She was wearing black sweats and looked even bigger, even bulkier than the other times I'd seen her.

"Isabelle," I breathed shakily. "Isabelle, it's you!"

Her normally neat, preppy style cast aside for unflattering fleece, she looked older and lumpish. Her face was a chalky white, her eyes wide with terror as real as mine.

"Where's Andy?" I asked.

"Wh-where's the money?" she demanded. But her voice cracked, as if it took her an enormous effort to demand anything of anyone.

I squinted at her. Was she bluffing? Did she really know where Andy was or if he was alive at all? I'd read about criminals who took advantage of a missing child, claimed they had kidnapped the kid then collected a ransom—even though they didn't have a clue where the kid was. But that didn't sound like mousey, meek Isabelle Vane.

I folded my arms across my chest in a show of authority. "I'm not paying you a cent until I know Andy's all right. I want to see him."

Isabelle's eyes misted over and she took a step backward, watching me warily. "I'll tell you where he is. He's not hurt, not badly that is." She must have seen the look of horror on my face. "I didn't mean to hurt him at all, honest. I just tapped him on the head to stun him a little."

"Tapped?" I asked, raising an eyebrow.

"Well, I had to knock him out so he'd fall into the trunk when he opened it. But he must have hit his nose on the metal hinge when he fell. He got a nosebleed. It just spurted everywhere." She sighed, gazing at me apologetically.

A rustle in the woods nearby caught Isabelle's attention. She turned and listened, her face rigid with concentration.

"It's nothing," I said quickly. "Just birds or a squirrel."

She turned back to me, looking even more nervous than before. "Give me the money, I'll tell you where your brother is."

"No," I said, standing firm.

Isabelle bit down on her bottom lip, looking worried. "No?"

"Not until you take me to him. As soon as I see for myself that he's all right, I'll give you the money and you can take off for South America, for all I care."

Her eyes flashed down to the bundle of bills in my hand, then up to my eyes, as if considering other options.

"If I wanted to take that money from you, you wouldn't have a chance against me," she said, her voice trembling.

I backed up hastily. She stepped forward, wearing a nervous expression.

She was an ox of a girl—no taller than me, but almost twice as heavy. She'd managed to shove Andy into the trunk of his car without any trouble, and she'd somehow gotten him out again before she ditched the Escort at the plantation. But if she grabbed the money and took off, we might never find Andy!

I jogged backward like a boxer, staying light on my feet to dodge quickly, keeping an eye on her hands, which, I'd noticed, seemed to give away her direction. Every time she took a step to the right, she opened her left hand and swung it across her body. Before she took her next step, she clenched and unclenched her fists several times.

She was clenching now. I sprung away from her, leading her toward open ground and the cinder track, where I'd be more visible.

"Joe, help!" I screamed.

Before I could turn and run, Isabelle bulldozed me to the hard, frosty ground. The air gushed out of my lungs as I hit the track and she smashed down on top

169

of me. Ripples of pain cut through my injured shoulder.

"Give it to me!" she screeched hysterically. "I'll kill you like I killed that cheating, horrible Miranda! I'll smash your skull in!"

I tried to shut out the pain while stuffing the wad of bills under my stomach, out of reach of her grasping hands.

"You want the money," I screamed, "take me to Andy!"

As we struggled on the cold ground, I was vaguely aware of a low, rumbling sound, growing louder. Suddenly we were caught in a brilliant splash of yellow light—the headlights of Joe's car.

Joe leaped on top of Isabelle, and all three of us were rolling on the ground—Isabelle cussing at us, kicking, and flailing with her big fists. One connected with the side of my head, and the football field spun in dark swirls around me.

From the edge of consciousness, I heard a voice shout, "Police! Freeze!"

A second later, the weight of two bodies lifted off of me, and I gasped for air. The tears came at once, hot and fast.

I lay on the ground, sobbing, cinders in my mouth and hair. Joe sat down beside me and pulled my head and shoulders into his lap. "You okay? Carrie, are you all right? Are you hurt bad?" he kept repeating.

In the background I could hear a woman's voice shouting at Isabelle, something about her rights, the usual TV stuff. I blinked away steamy tears and stared in amazement at the gray-haired hag in a baggy coat who was slapping handcuffs on Isabelle.

* * *

"I haven't done anything wrong!" Isabelle protested tearfully twenty minutes later, when we were all back at the police station. "I was just taking a shortcut across the field, and these two jumped me! It was horrible!"

"Isabelle attacked Carrie," Joe said, his voice icy cold with anger. "She's hidden Andy somewhere, and she wanted money for him."

"She admitted killing Miranda," I added, looking urgently at Red.

She'd taken off the old lady disguise she'd worn to tail me when an unmarked car had become too obvious. Now she perched on one corner of a table in the interrogation room where we all sat, while Toup sat in the corner, hunched over a tape recorder and his trusty notebook.

"She told me how she'd kidnapped Andy from the parking lot. The blood was from his nose; he hit it on the car when he fell," I said.

Isabelle rolled her eyes. "They're making all of this up."

Red turned her attention away from me, back to Isabelle. "It seems we have a difference of opinion here."

Isabelle studied her warily. "I'm telling the truth. I don't know why anyone should think I'd kill some girl I hardly knew."

Red nodded thoughtfully.

I figured all was lost and dropped my head into my hands.

"Then how did you get the paintings from Vivaldi's Collectibles?" Red asked after a minute.

Isabelle scowled at her suspiciously. "I . . . I never went into that store."

Liar, I thought. *You told me you'd tutored Miranda there.*

"But you did sell paintings from that shop to another store in Annapolis, and Mrs. Hemingway never authorized such a sale."

Red opened a folder on her desk and produced a typed statement along with what looked like three receipts.

Isabelle's eyes flicked, desperately around the room.

I stared at Red with new appreciation, realizing she must have somehow followed me to Annapolis, then taken up the lead I'd thought was a dead end. She must have believed in me!

The sergeant's green cat eyes shifted once in my direction, in a not unfriendly way, then back to her suspect.

Isabelle chewed her bottom lip. "It was Miranda's idea," she blurted out, her eyes dark and moving constantly as she sought for safe words. "She told me she'd pay me to make copies of a few paintings. It would be like practicing, you know, working on my brush techniques."

"So you didn't know you were doing anything wrong," Red stated sympathetically.

"Not at first," Isabelle insisted.

I gripped the edge of my chair, thinking, *Well, this is great. Now we know Miranda and Isabelle were pulling some kind of scam. But what about my brother? Where is he?* I wanted to scream. *Why was this taking so long?*

I leaned forward and started to open my mouth as Isabelle continued talking and a silent Toup took notes. Red shot me a look that said, *Wait!*

"I was just doing the copies for fun, and a little cash," Isabelle said. "I made enough to buy my class

172

ring, then enough to get myself some really nice art supplies. It was great!" Her eyes sparkled.

"Then what?" Red asked.

"Then I found out Miranda was selling the original paintings in Baltimore, and leaving the ones I'd painted in her aunt's store. You know, to cover up her stealing the real ones. Her aunt couldn't tell the difference between the real ones and the fakes!" Isabelle said.

"So you told her you wouldn't do any more," Red supplied.

Isabelle nodded emphatically. "Of course. But she threatened me. She said if I wouldn't keep on painting for her, she'd go to the police and tell them she'd discovered forgeries in her aunt's shop. She needed money for costumes, you see, and for an expensive dance coach in New York City. She didn't want me to stop as long as she kept getting hundreds of dollars for each painting."

I leaned across the table again. "You two had an argument at the antique store."

"Yes," Isabelle admitted sadly. "I had to work there because we couldn't take the paintings out of Vivaldi's without risking her aunt missing them. I finally had enough of Miranda's threats. She wanted me to do more and more paintings. It was stupid—if we kept it up, sooner or later we'd be sure to get caught. And she was greedy, so very greedy . . ." Isabelle melted into a pool of tears. "I didn't hurt her . . . I *didn't* . . . we just argued, that's all . . ."

"You *did* hurt her," Red said firmly. She reached into a brown grocery bag that sat on the floor beside her and pulled out a dark green jade bookend wrapped in clear plastic. When she set it on the table with a heavy thud, Isabelle's eyes widened. "This is what you used to hit Miranda over the head. *This* is what you used to kill her."

I started to say, *But there were no fingerprints! You said they were wiped off of everything!* Red's eyes flickered a warning at me, as if she knew what I was thinking.

But Isabelle jumped in before I could say anything. "No!" she cried. "There couldn't be any prints or blood! You're lying! I washed them off and . . ." Her eyes widened in horror as Toup and Red exchanged triumphant glances. "Oh, no," she gasped. "Oh, no . . ."

I couldn't wait any longer. "Andy," I said, seizing Isabelle's hand where it rested on the table. "Where is he, Isabelle?"

She didn't respond.

"Please, now that it's all out in the open, tell us where my brother is."

She pulled her hand out of mine and dropped her head onto her arms. "Miranda was such a terrible girl. She was mean to everyone. She deserved to die."

"I know, I know . . . but *Andy* doesn't."

"What does it matter?" she muttered miserably into her sweatshirt sleeves. "Nothing matters."

I shot a panicky look at Red.

She sighed. "Maybe you and Joe had better leave now. Let us talk to her, maybe we can . . ."

"No!" I cried. I could sense Isabelle shutting herself off from us, as if she realized she'd admitted too much already and anything more she said would only get her into deeper trouble.

I shot up out of my chair, knocking it over backward as I launched myself across the table at her. She tensed and pulled away, but I was able to grab the front of her sweatshirt. I shook her good and hard, and Red didn't stop me.

"You know where my brother is!" I growled in her face. "*You know!* If you tell us right now, the police will go easier on you."

"Now, Carrie—" Red began.

"No!" I shouted at her. Maybe she was a good cop and she'd done her job by finding Miranda's killer, but my family's nightmare wouldn't be over until Andy was home and safe. "It's true, isn't it?" I demanded. "When someone cooperates with the police, helps them recover a kidnap victim, the court often gives them a shorter sentence, right?"

"Kidnapping is a federal offense," Toup commented darkly.

Isabelle's eyes widened in terror.

Red glared at her partner. It was a dumb thing to say. He might as well have told Isabelle she'd been smart to play innocent.

"Wait!" I cried. "If Andy is found and he's okay, maybe no kidnapping charges will be filed."

Isabelle looked at me questioningly, then at the cops. "Is that possible?"

"Anything you can do to cooperate, especially if it means saving a life, will be held in your favor," Red said guardedly.

Isabelle dried her eyes and thought for a moment. "I'll tell you where to find Andy," she said at last.

"This is the place," Red said as Toup stopped the police cruiser in front of an abandoned apartment building off of York Road.

Windows were broken out on all three floors, and some wannabe artist had spraypainted swirly initials and slogans across the dirty red brick.

"This place was supposed to have been pulled down weeks ago," Toup said.

The car had barely rolled to a standstill when I tried to open the door from the backseat. I couldn't find a handle or release for the lock.

"Hold your horses," Red said gruffly.

But there was a softness in her tone and her eyes that hadn't been there when I'd first met her.

I could guess what she was thinking—that she didn't want me to be there when they went down into the basement of the abandoned apartment house where Isabelle said she'd left Andy. He'd had no food or water for days, and the nights had been bitterly cold.

I swallowed and reached for Joe's hand as we ran up the cracked sidewalk, Red in the lead, Toup bringing up the rear with a high-intensity electric torch and a boltcutter.

Red circled around to the back and stopped in front of a slanted metal storm door secured with a padlock. "Call out to him," she said, "so he knows we're the good guys."

"Andy?" My voice shook uncontrollably. I sniffled back tears. "Andy, please answer me. Are you all right?"

There was no answer.

"What if he's not here?" Joe whispered.

Red ignored him. "Cut the lock," she ordered Toup.

I pressed close to the door as Red's partner positioned the strong jaws of the boltcutter on the stem of the lock. "Andy! Andy, it's Carrie. We're getting you out of there!"

Metal cracked loudly in the night, and the padlock fell with a clatter on the cement sidewalk. Toup lifted the door, revealing a short flight of steps that led below ground level.

"I'll go first," Red said, shining the torch down the concrete stairs.

I followed close behind her. There was a second door at the bottom, but it wasn't locked. The smell of mildew, damp rot, and something sickeningly sweet wafted up at me. Something that reminded me of a dead mouse we'd found in a heating duct at the studio.

"I really think you should stay here," Red repeated. She looked at Joe. "It would be better for her."

"No," I snapped, pushing past her into an open cellar. The cement floor was littered with trash, and iron columns ran up to cobwebby timbers that crossed the low ceiling. An old washing machine and dryer, with coin slots like at the laundromat, stood against one wall. Along another were storage bins, divided into cagelike sections. They had probably been used by tenants to store their personal things.

The bins were all empty now, except for one. A dark lump lay in the far end, and it took a moment for me to recognize it as a person, curled up in a tight ball on the filthy floor.

"There!" I cried, grabbing Red's hand and swinging her torch around to shine its yellow beam on the lump. "Andy! Andy!"

Grabbing the boltcutters from Toup, I ran at the wire mesh door and chomped down on the bicycle lock looping its frame.

Andy rolled onto his side as I ran through the door. Dropping to my knees, I reached out to hug him. He gently pushed me away and looked up at me, his eyes bleary and unfocused, his lips cracked, face pale.

"What took you so freakin' long?" he rasped in disgust, then grinned at me.

17

*A week later, Andy's appe-*tite was back to normal and he was in school.

He'd pretended to be tough when we found him, insisting on walking without help out to the police cruiser. But anyone could see how wobbly his steps were, how he reached out to touch the cement walls of the stairwell as we climbed from the basement into the fresh night air.

Red had insisted on taking him straight to the hospital. The doctor wasn't sure how much longer Andy would have survived. He was weak from dehydration and days of exposure to the cold. I was just glad we'd found him.

My parents refused to press charges against Isabelle since she'd told the police where Andy was. I don't think they ever realized how close she'd come to sticking to her story that she knew nothing about his disappearance. They never saw the basement where she'd left him to rot.

Unfortunately for her, the Baltimore County District Attorney's office refused to lower the first-degree murder charge. They called her killing of Miranda cruel, brutal, and unprovoked. Obviously they hadn't known Miranda.

Three more weeks passed, and my shoulder was almost as good as new, but I couldn't forget about all that had happened. Sometimes I'd wake up in the middle of the night, screaming, convinced that a two-ton mermaid was falling on me. Other times I had horrible, chilling nightmares about being shut in the dank basement where we'd found Andy. I swear I could feel rats scurrying across my body as I lay, curled up on the dusty cement floor. Then we heard that the building had been demolished by a wrecking crew, and I wondered if anyone had bothered to check the basement before bringing the three floors above it crashing down.

At last it was time for the Mid-Atlantic Ballroom comps.

I looked around, my thoughts still tangled up in Miranda, Isabelle, Andy and myself as music swelled around me. A dozen couples in glittering costumes whirled across the room.

The Hilton ballroom was much larger than the floor at the studio. Surrounded by tables occupied by other dancers waiting for their turn on the floor, and a wildly applauding audience, the place looked more like a movie set for a royal ball than a Baltimore hotel.

"What are you thinking about, Carrie?" my partner asked.

"Who, not what," I said. Turning around, I smiled up at Joe. "I was thinking about Isabelle and Miranda."

Andy had stuck with his decision not to dance in

the Mid-Atlantics with me, or with anyone else. But I was sort of glad. I'd had a lot of fun training Joe, or trying to train him. He was about as cooperative and disciplined as a puppy. He liked to do things *his* way.

I knew we didn't have a chance of winning our category. But that was okay, I'd decided. I hadn't been this relaxed at a comp since I was a little kid. Today, we'd dance just for fun.

"What about Isabelle and Miranda?" he asked.

"Just the way it all happened," I said with a shrug. A couple whipped past us, their faces plastered with forced smiles for the cameras and judges. When Joe and I danced, I knew my smile would be real. "Isabelle claims Miranda was the one who broke into the studio and stole my gown and tapes."

"So?"

"So, I'd assumed that it had to have been someone else who took my stuff. You know, because then it turned up in my locker after Miranda was dead."

"But Isabelle knew she'd taken it and decided to confuse the evidence by ditching it in your locker," Joe reasoned.

"Right, that would make anything else I told the police sound less believable, because they'd think I'd made up the story about someone breaking in and stealing my dress. Isabelle must have been desperate to steer the police away from her. She must have known about my argument in school earlier that day with Miranda. I was the perfect suspect." I thought for a minute. "Then there was the paintbrush."

"What about it?"

"Isabelle must have come back to Vivaldi's, looking for stuff she'd left behind, like the brush."

"But you interrupted her search."

"Right," I said. "She suspected then that I might be getting close to the truth. When she saw me with the brush, she panicked and pushed the figurehead over on me."

Joe sighed. "She's a really talented artist, too. It's too bad she went off the deep end like that."

I nodded. "Yeah. You know, I don't think it would have gone that badly for her with the police if she'd just gone to them and told them what had happened that night. I'll bet Isabelle was just scared and lashed out. Killing Miranda was probably an accident."

Isabelle's lawyer had taken things even further, claiming she'd acted in self-defense. Miranda, he said, had picked up the bookend first and attacked Isabelle. Since there were no fingerprints, it would be hard to prove who had picked up the murder weapon first. I didn't know what to believe, but it was clear that after Miranda was dead, Isabelle had become greedy and decided she deserved some of the money Miranda had been getting for the paintings.

But things had gotten out of hand. She'd had to devise more and more ways to make it seem that someone else had killed Miranda. And I was the perfect scapegoat. She admitted that taking Andy hostage wasn't such a good idea. She'd only intended to keep him a day or so, as a way of finally convincing the police that I was behind everything.

The public address system crackled after the music stopped. I reached out for Joe's hand and squeezed it.

"Dancers for the Junior International Modern Competition, on the floor, please," the announcer boomed.

Joe leaned over and kissed me quickly, then grinned. "That's us!"

"Break a leg, partner," I murmured, my heart racing as we walked quickly to the middle of the floor and took dance position.

He winked at me. ''I thought this wasn't a contact sport.''

I giggled. ''It is, the way you dance,'' I teased.

Oh, by the way—we took second place!

NIGHTMARES

DARK VISIONS
by L.J. Smith

"Read their minds. Steal their souls. Take your pick."

He was standing very still, every muscle rigid. His hands were shoved in his pockets, fingers clenched. And his grey eyes were so bleak and lonely that Kaitlyn was glad he wasn't looking at her.

She said evenly, "You're a telepath."

"They called it something different. They called me a psychic vampire."

And I felt sorry for myself, Kaitlyn thought. Just because I couldn't help people, because my drawings were useless. But his gift makes him kill.

DARK VISIONS
Book One: *The Secret Power*
Book Two: *The Passion*
Book Three: *The Possessed*

By the author of *The Vampire Diaries* and *The Forbidden Game* trilogy.

SUMMER'S END

by Robert Hawks

It was happening, Amy knew it.

In a moment the vampire would return and this time Amy knew there would be no hesitation; this time he would strike and she would be taken in an instant. It would be over, and that was what sent her jumping through the window, into the sand outside and running down to the beach.

Where to go? What to do? She was in her bare feet, stumbling across rock and twig and sand... not that she expected to make it anyway – there was a vampire behind her, after all...

" The panther knew she dreamed of him every night,
and the knowledge made him powerful.
He knew she thought about him even when she
was awake. Somehow, Holly was sure he knew it.
The panther knew she ate raw meat and licked the
blood from her lips…"

Year of the Cat
The terrifying new trilogy by Zoe Daniels

BOOK ONE: *THE DREAM*
When Holly Callison arrives at Los Gatos High
School, she learns more than the legend of the panther.
She unlocks the secret of her nightmares, the hunger in
her soul – and the savage nature of her true self.

BOOK TWO: *THE HUNT*
As Holly explores the wild side of her secret destiny,
she fears for the lives of the people she loves. But still,
she cannot resist the power of the ancient rituals – and
the bloodthirsty call of the hunt.

BOOK THREE: *THE AMULET*
In terror and desperation, Holly tries to cling to her
human side. But the blood of the panther runs wild in
her veins. And soon she's forced to choose sides – in the
final war between predator and prey.

Order Form

To order books direct from the publishers, just make a list of the titles you want and send it with your name and address to:

Dept 6,
HarperCollins Publishers Ltd,
Westerhill Road,
Bishopbriggs,
Glasgow G64 2QT

Please enclose a cheque or postal order to the value of the cover price, plus:

UK and BFPO: Add £1 for the first book, and 25p per copy for each additional book ordered.

Overseas and Eire: Add £2.95 service charge. Books will be sent by surface mail, but quotes for airmail despatch will be given on request.

A 24-hour telephone ordering service is available to Visa and Access card holders on 0141-772 2281.